ABDUCTION

A.C. JETT

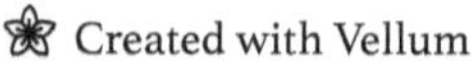 Created with Vellum

1

———

At the close of an intimate dinner party, Josh and Amy stood outside their Topanga Canyon cabin, bidding farewell to their two departing medical student friends, Teddy and Pam.

Josh, a charismatic twenty-something with a love for music and humor, put an arm around his fiancée, Amy, a radiant young woman in her early twenties. In the quiet calm of the night, the sounds of laughter and conversation faded as their guest's car headlights disappeared down the driveway.

The couple looked up at the ink-black sky littered with twinkling stars. Josh leaned over, planting a soft kiss on Amy's cheek, just as a shooting star whizzed across their field of vision, paused, and then shot straight upwards.

"Did you see that?" Amy asked in awe, her eyes still tracing the star's path.

"Shooting star," Josh replied with a chuckle.

"It zoomed straight up."

"Comet."

"Not like that," she said.

"Satellite."

"You're crazy."

A warm Santa Ana wind swept over them, carrying their laughter into the night.

Later, in their bedroom, Josh placed his money clip and a gold Cross pen atop an oak dresser beside the fireplace. Beside it, a goldfish swam peacefully in its tiny bowl. Josh, dressed in a UCLA T-shirt and shorts, fell into bed beside his saxophone and played a few sultry notes. Amy, wearing a Stanford sweatshirt, curled up next to him, and they wrapped their arms around each other. She clasped Josh's hand, showing off her new diamond engagement ring under the soft light.

"Thank you," she whispered.

"Was it a nice surprise?" Josh asked.

"I loved having old friends drop by for this special occasion. And it's nice to be down for the weekend. I wish I could do it more often."

"It was romantic, though, wasn't it?"

"How am I going to tell my Dad? Yes, your honor. I'm marrying a musician."

"He'll kill you. Then he'll throw me in jail for murder."

"That's what I like about you. Always positive."

Amy smiled and pulled him in for a passionate kiss.

"I can't breathe," Josh managed to say between gasps.

"But can you still blow your horn?" Amy teased, passing him his saxophone.

As the notes of *Out of Nowhere* filled the room, Amy's laughter followed him under the covers. The music started, stopped, and then started again, the saxophone becoming a playful part of their bedtime ritual. They fell into a comfortable silence, their bodies entwined as they drifted into dreamland.

The silence of the night was interrupted only by the ticking of a digital clock that read 3:13 a.m. in ominous, blood-red numerals. A hot breeze billowed the curtains, rousing Amy from her slumber. She sat upright, heart pounding, skin crawling with an unshakable dread.

"Josh, did you lock the door?" she whispered anxiously into the quiet room.

"It's locked," Josh mumbled sleepily, not bothering to open his eyes.

Despite his assurances, Amy couldn't shake the feeling of unease that gnawed at her. She picked up a baseball bat for reassurance and tiptoed into the living room, checking the front door. It was locked and deadbolted, just as Josh had said. Slightly relieved, she returned to the bedroom.

The room looked different now, somehow otherworldly. Pockets of light danced on the ceiling while shadows performed a mysterious ballet. As Amy rubbed her eyes, trying to make sense of the vision, she noticed three short gray figures huddled around the bed.

A gasp caught in her throat as she realized the figures were not figments of her imagination. The grays, uncannily similar to the ones she had read about in alien conspiracies, surrounded Josh. One of them turned towards Amy, its vast, black, vacant eyes penetrating her soul. Her grip on the baseball bat faltered, the weapon clattering to the floor.

"Josh, Josh, wake up. Please, Josh," she pleaded, but her voice seemed to echo in a void.

As she backed against the wall, the scent of the alien leader, gamy and pungent, filled the room. She heard a hollow, sinister voice inside her head, the alien's thin lips never moving. "Do not be afraid."

"Who are you? What do you want?" Amy asked, terror evident in her voice.

"We will not hurt you," was the emotionless reply.

When the alien touched her with its sickly appendage, she winced at its chilling touch. Her engagement ring caught the light and reflected in its vast black eyes. Suddenly, to her horror, she started floating off the floor.

"Nooo. This isn't happening. Tell me this is a dream. Josh, Josh, please wake up. Help me!" she screamed.

Despite her pleas, the alien creatures seized her and began to move past the fireplace. In a desperate attempt, Amy grabbed Josh's gold pen and swiped at the air. The sudden commotion stirred Josh awake. He saw the baseball bat, forced himself to his feet, and lifted it above his head.

But before he could strike, the alien leader turned on him, his gaze filled with ancient rage. With a simple motion of his hand, Josh's screams were silenced. His eyes widened, and he crashed to the floor, knocking over the goldfish bowl in his fall. The fish flopped onto the carpet, gasping for breath.

Amy watched in horror as the merciless abductors led her away. Her last glimpse of Josh was through the bedroom door before she and the gray aliens seemed to dissolve through the dark cabin wall, disappearing as though the wall was not there.

2

The morning dawned bright and beautiful. Sparrows trilled from the trees, their cheerful songs filling the cabin as daylight streamed through the window. Josh stirred from a deep slumber, the familiar weight of Amy's hand resting on his chest. As he lifted her hand, he noticed her ring was missing. He glanced at the clock, which read 10:30 a.m.

"Shit!" he muttered, springing up from the bed and making a beeline for the bathroom.

The cold water he splashed on his face did little to wake him up. His eyes scanned the mirror as he turned on the shower, noticing a small gash on his forehead. He called out, "Amy, do you know what time it is?"

Back in the bedroom, he threw on a shirt, a button snapping off in his haste. "Oh, shit!" he exclaimed again. He glanced at the bed. Amy still hadn't moved. "Amy? Honey, wake up," he called, but she didn't respond. Her eyes were wide open, dilated in terror, and utterly still.

"God, Amy!" Josh whispered, terror seizing his heart.

. . .

An hour later, the cabin was buzzing with paramedics and police. Crime scene tape was strung around the property's perimeter, a grim testament to the tragedy.

A green Plymouth Fury skidded into the dust, disgorging two men. The first, Matt Steel, a seasoned LAPD homicide detective in his mid-thirties. His eyes held a world-weary cynicism, the chiseled lines of his face reflecting a life shaped by danger and pain. His partner, Buddy Zeppo, was a stark contrast to him, with a boyish, chubby face and a clumsy demeanor.

"Bedroom?" Matt asked a uniformed cop, who replied, "This is thirteen, Matt."

Matt shrugged off the cop's attempt to rattle him and entered the bedroom. The sight that greeted him was horrific. Amy's lifeless eyes were wide open, frozen in terror. Matt reached out and gently closed them.

"Pretty," he muttered, and the cop retorted, "If dead's your type."

"Same M.O. as the rest," the cop added as Matt examined the room. "Young, innocent. No sign of forced entry."

"Find anything?" Matt asked.

In the cabin's dim, dappled light, a cop thumbed through a pile of songs and sheet music. "Just these notes," he declared, his voice matter-of-fact.

"No sign of struggle. Just like the others," Matt concluded, his eyes falling on the saxophone and sheet music.

"Was she alone?" he asked, his voice holding a hint of heaviness.

"No," the cop replied, shaking his head. "Her boyfriend's a songwriter. He's outside, singing the blues."

"He got a name?" Matt inquired, maintaining a calm, dispassionate demeanor.

"Yeah, but no record," the cop responded tersely.

Matt grimaced. It was going to be a long day.

· · ·

The cabin's porch was warm and inviting, but Josh couldn't appreciate its charm as he stared blankly at the nearby forest and the neighboring cabin. His eyes held a hollowed look as Detective Matt Steel approached.

Matt flashed his LAPD badge at Josh, staring at the nearby forest and a neighboring cabin. "Matt Steel, LAPD," he introduced himself, "Your fish died." Despite the odd pronouncement, Josh remained silent, his gaze steady. "Must be nice living out here. Beats the hell out of the city. I hate pollution. You smoke?" Matt lit up a Marlboro and offered one to Josh, but he passed.

"Do you have more questions?" Josh finally responded, his voice heavy with resignation. "I already answered the guys inside."

"Only if you're willing to talk about it," Matt countered, keeping his gaze on the quiet man. "Tell me again. From the start."

"We went to bed. Everything was fine," Josh offered in a near whisper.

"But there was no water in the fishbowl," Matt observed cryptically, a statement that earned him a puzzled look from Josh.

"I woke up. She was just there," Josh admitted, his face a blank slate.

"Papa bear. Not too hot, not too cold," Matt tossed out, trying to inject some levity into the somber exchange. "Goldilocks and The Three Bears. I'll huff, I'll puff and blow your house down," he added, interpreting Josh's confused expression. As he spoke, two burly cops strolled by.

"Those were pigs," Josh corrected him, his voice laced with annoyance.

"At least you've got your stories straight. You two have a fight?" Matt shifted gears, his gaze scrutinizing.

"No," Josh responded, his eyes drifting away from Matt's.

"What did you talk about?" Matt pressed, pushing for details.

"Nothing. We had friends over for dinner," Josh divulged, watching as Matt extracted a notebook and scanned its contents.

"Yeah, Teddy and Pam Worden," Matt read aloud, keeping his gaze on Josh.

"Yes," Josh confirmed.

"We talked to them. They claimed they weren't here," Matt revealed casually.

"That's impossible. We had dinner together," Josh refuted, his voice laced with panic.

"They're at a medical conference in San Francisco," Matt countered, a touch of triumph in his voice.

"They were here," Josh insisted, desperation creeping into his tone.

"For the last three days, they've been at UCSF," Matt informed him.

"That's bullshit. They were here last night. They're my friends," Josh protested, his voice quivering.

Casually discarding his cigarette, Matt stepped closer to Josh. "So, what did you use, Josh? Pills, gas. Something kinky? I'll find out anyway."

"I didn't use anything," Josh defended.

"You strangled her with your bare hands, didn't you?" Matt accused, his tone ruthless.

"No," Josh denied.

"A pillow on the head. That always works," Matt speculated coldly.

"No!" Josh roared, his voice echoing off the surrounding quiet.

"I know. You killed her with one of your songs," Matt insisted, his voice ice-cold.

"No, no, no. I was asleep. I don't remember anything. I don't know what happened," Josh spat out, his voice shaking with the weight of his denial.

"Let me tell you about guys who blackout after these kinds of murders, Josh," Matt said, his tone hardening. "At first, they forget, but pretty soon, they start remembering. And fast." Matt informed him, his voice even. "Last night, everything was fine. This morning, you wake up next to a dead woman. Think about it." His words hung in the air, leaving Josh with his thoughts and fears.

Josh was at a loss. He couldn't remember anything. He felt his legs giving way, and he crumbled to the steps, holding his stomach.

"Go ahead. Cry, pee, throw up. Nothing makes me sick," Matt said with a trace of indifference. He knelt beside Josh and warned him about the possibility of sudden memories years after the murder.

Josh continued to insist that he didn't do it, but Matt had seen enough. He signaled for Zeppo to cuff Josh, reading him his rights as they escorted him to the waiting Plymouth Fury.

3

———

In a sterile police interview room, Matt and Zeppo stared down at Josh in an intense standoff. The room was sparse, with only a table and a few chairs. The occupants' fatigue was apparent, a sign of a prolonged interrogation.

"Okay. Now, tell me this part again. What did you have for dinner?" Matt asked, the weariness in his voice evident.

"Clam linguini," Josh responded, his voice almost a whisper.

"And a burgundy wine?" Matt questioned further.

"Yes, and Caesar salad," Josh added, his gaze fixed on the table's wood grain.

"The two don't go together. You always want a white wine with a nice linguini," Zeppo chimed in, earning a side glance from Matt.

His curiosity piqued, Matt asked, "What kind of dressing did she have on her salad?"

The shrug was almost audible in Josh's gruff voice, "French, Italian... I don't know. What the fuck do you want from me? I don't remember."

Matt pounced, his words coming out sharp. "You fuck her?"

"I want an attorney," Josh replied, his voice growing strained.

"It's easy to find out. You did, didn't you?" Matt insisted, an almost gloating note coloring his tone.

"No. I want out of here now." Josh was losing his composure.

"You fucked her, then you killed her. Right? Just like the other twelve. We know what you did, Josh. So, just say it," Matt accused him, his voice growing fiercer.

"No. I loved Amy. We just got engaged. I gave her a ring," Josh protested, his voice a desperate whisper. "She had a ring on her finger."

"Really?" Matt questioned, skepticism evident in his tone. He glanced at Zeppo, who shook his head. There was no ring.

Minutes later, inside a private viewing room, Matt flipped through the case files and conferred with his partner. Through the one-way mirror, they could see Josh.

"Twelve guys. Twelve victims, no witnesses. Same song and dance. Now they're all back on the street, and we're looking like bozos," Matt muttered, frustration pouring out in every word.

"I hate liars," Zeppo commented as he watched Josh from the cubicle. He wore his usual black and white checkered jacket, green polyester shirt, and dull orange permanent-press pants. His stomach strained against the fabric as he pulled it in.

"No family, no friends. No past," Matt added, his tone thoughtful.

"You think this guy did it?" Zeppo asked, his gaze never leaving Josh.

"I get the feeling he knows who did, and he's covering for him," Matt answered, his words filled with certainty.

Zeppo let out a long sigh, his disbelief evident as he stated,

"A beautiful girl with a psycho when there are so many cute guys around."

In the bustling hallway of the police station, Emily Mist, a street-smart, Cambridge-educated tabloid photojournalist in her mid-thirties, weaved her way through a group of cops. As she moved, heads turned, their eyes following her confident stride. Stopping in her tracks as her gaze met Matt's, an intense look of recognition passed between them.

Emily was not a woman who was easily pushed around. She had an unmistakable allure, an unshakable gaze that unsettled Matt, an enticing perfume that gently announced her presence, and a tough yet sexual demeanor. She was pretty, all class, and a woman who commanded attention.

"I smell history in the making," Zeppo said, his voice filled with intrigue. He drifted away, leaving Matt and Emily in a charged air of intensity. Matt's face had a certain hardness, a hint of pain, and bad memories.

"What brings you here? A crashed UFO or Elvis's ghost?" Matt asked, his tone caustic.

"Invisible killer rapes pregnant women in their sleep," Emily retorted, her British accent wrapping around each word. There was a playful yet determined glare in her eyes.

"Haven't seen him."

"Heard you finally caught the guy," Emily countered, her gaze unyielding.

"Rumors," Matt retorted dismissively.

"They say you've got a dozen cuties in the morgue and a trail that leads to the sky," she challenged.

"The evidence is piling up," he admitted, his voice flat.

"So is the B.S. I hear you're looking for witnesses?" Emily shot back, a hint of a smirk playing on her lips.

"Reliable witnesses. You wouldn't know any," he retorted,

his words sharp.

"Don't bet on it," she fired back.

Inside the viewing room, Emily spotted Josh. She quickly pulled out her 35-SLR Nikon from her case and shot off a few frames before Matt could stop her.

"Prime suspect?" she asked, keeping her gaze on Josh.

"Very prime," Matt responded, his voice barely more than a grunt.

"He didn't do it," Emily declared, her tone assertive.

"No. Of course not. Only you would know that. Who do you think it was this time, some international terrorist or the hillside strangler?" Matt shot back, his voice dripping with sarcasm.

"You never listen, do you? You want my statement or not?" Emily asked, a hint of defiance in her voice. The air in the room was electric as the battle of wills between the two continued.

In the sterile confines of the interrogation room, Josh paced anxiously, etching nervous paths into the worn linoleum. As the door opened, Matt, Zeppo, and Emily filed in.

"Josh? I'm Emily Mist, Amy's neighbor. I live next door," Emily introduced herself, her voice filled with warmth.

"I'm screwed, aren't I?" Josh responded, a mix of fear and resignation in his voice.

"Careful, kid. You're talking to a reporter," Matt cautioned, a stern look in his eyes.

Emily quickly intervened, "I heard your friends leaving last night. You talked about stars."

"See," Josh exclaimed, pointing towards Emily as if she was his proof of his innocence. Matt looked at her, his skepticism evident.

"Tell me, what happened?" Emily asked, her gaze soft but probing.

"Off the record?" Josh asked, his eyes darting between Emily and Matt.

"Yeah," Emily reassured him.

"I don't know. They think I killed Amy. I didn't," he admitted, his voice barely a whisper.

Turning to Matt, Emily questioned, "You pressing charges?"

"Soon," he responded curtly.

"Then, he's free to go?" Emily asked, a glimmer of hope in her voice.

"But not too far," Matt warned as he stepped out of their way.

"Keep up the excellent work, detective," Emily said, her tone laced with irony. She left with Josh, leaving Matt and Zeppo behind.

"You letting those legs walk out on you again?" Zeppo asked, his eyes fixated on Emily's retreating figure.

"Zepp, there's more to a woman than her departure," Matt retorted, his eyes following Emily's exit.

Later, in a Hollywood café, the clatter of plates filled the air, and envious glances from people without housing outside pierced through the windows. After a frustrating phone call, Josh joined Emily in a quiet booth, his food untouched.

"I take it that didn't go well," Emily commented, her gaze sympathetic.

"He said I must be smoking something. He said they weren't there," Josh replied in a hopeless tone.

"Men in black," Emily said.

"What?"

"They got to them. It happens all the time."

As they discussed further, he confessed, "I don't know what to do. I can't believe this is happening. I can't believe she's gone."

Emily reassured him, "Josh, this may be hard for you, but I know Matt. I've known him for a long time. I know how he thinks. He's very tough. He won't let it rest. Can you remember anything?"

The conversation suddenly turned when Josh recalled, "Owls, owls over the lake... snarling dogs, owls over the lake, their faces ripped from their masks."

"What?"

"It's part of a song I wrote. I think I had a dream about owls," he added, suddenly standing up, his eyes wild with the revelation.

"There was no music," he added, quickly sketching the rough image of an owl with large dark eyes on a napkin.

"Owls?"

"Yeah."

Two men in black suits entered the coffee shop.

"There's someone we should talk to," she said.

Josh and Emily hurried out, leaving the owl sketch behind on the diner napkin. The strangers picked it up.

In the calming ambiance of a hypnotherapist's office, Emily and Josh were greeted by Dr. Medea, a friendly, professional-looking woman in her mid-fifties.

"Josh, this is Dr. Medea. I think she can help us find out what happened last night," Emily introduced, gesturing towards the comforting figure of the hypnotherapist.

Meanwhile, back at Matt Steel's office, the shrill ring of the telephone cut through the silence. Zeppo trotted over and picked up the receiver. "Homicide? Yeah, just a minute," he muttered into the device before covering the mouthpiece. "Your old heartthrob. The legs that go on forever," he quipped, passing the call to Matt.

"Steel here," Matt greeted, his voice smooth and composed.

"You're never going to believe this. I've got something," Emily's voice echoed from the other end.

"If you start every sentence telling me I'm never going to believe it, you're right. I won't," Matt retorted, leaning back in his chair.

"Matt, this is serious," Emily pressed her tone sterner this time.

"I know. You got a full confession signed in blood, right?" Matt quipped, a smirk playing on his lips.

"Better than that," Emily replied, her voice filled with excitement.

As the conversation continued, Emily brought up a new lead. "Look, wise guy. Josh's pen is missing."

"What a shame. That'll put a flat note in his songwriting career," Matt responded, failing to grasp the gravity of the situation.

"Your men must have overlooked it at the crime scene," Emily continued, her voice a little exasperated. "He carried that pen with him twenty-four hours a day for the last ten years," she explained, hoping Matt would understand its significance.

"I know it's been a long time since we talked, Emily, but I'm not in charge of supplies anymore," Matt responded, his tone laced with sarcasm.

"Just check it out. If you look carefully by the fireplace in the cabin, you'll find it in the wall," Emily finally instructed before abruptly hanging up.

"A pen in the wall," Matt mused, getting up from his chair.

"She solve a piece of the puzzle?" Zeppo asked, looking over at his partner.

"I think she's encouraging me to improve my note-taking," Matt responded, chuckling at the thought.

4

———

Inside the cozy cabin bedroom of the crime scene, Matt worked diligently on a section of the pine wall marked with a circular chalk outline. He drilled a hole, used a jigsaw to gouge the wall, and finally extracted a cylindrical core section.

"A psychic help you on this one?" Matt teased Emily, who was capturing the scene with her camera. She looked softer and more approachable in the warm daylight that filtered through the window.

"Something like that," she replied calmly, focusing her camera lens.

"The Star's been good to you?" Matt continued the small talk, a glint of curiosity in his eyes.

"Right up there with being a cop," Emily replied, smiling.

"But there is one difference. I get the facts. You make them up," Matt retorted, not missing a beat.

"No one expects the law to place a premium on creativity, Matt, especially for someone who couldn't pass woodshop," Emily fired back, her eyes still fixated on her camera.

Matt carefully removed the wood core through the wall-board and smiled.

They relocated to a forensic lab later in the day. A technician returned with the woodcut and an X-ray and slid the pictures onto the view box. He flipped the light switch on, illuminating the outline of the gold Cross pen inside the wood grain.

"There," Emily pointed, her eyes gleaming with satisfaction.

"You mind elaborating on the significance of this?" Matt asked, trying to connect the dots.

"He carries it with him all the time," Emily stated.

"I know, twenty-four hours a day. Ten years. Waiting for a Top 40 hit. How did it get inside the wall?" Matt questioned, his curiosity piqued.

"Amy must have put it there in her sleep," Emily suggested, to which Matt responded with sarcasm: "Why didn't I think of that? Inside a wall, it's a perfect place to hide your boyfriend's pen, don't you agree, chief?"

"I don't think so," the technician interjected, pointing at the X-ray. "This pen wasn't put there, detective, last night. Or the night before."

"Okay, when was it put there?" Matt asked, trying to make sense of the unfolding mystery.

"See these rings in the wood. This pen has been in there for fifty, maybe sixty years," the technician explained.

"The cabins were only built thirty years ago," Emily intervened, frowning at the conundrum.

"Look, I'm just telling you what I see," the technician shrugged, unfazed.

"Maybe the tree was fifty years old when they cut it down?" Matt suggested, searching for a rational explanation.

"True, but the odd thing is there's no fiber disruption," the technician added, "This pen couldn't have been placed there last night or a hundred years ago. There's no cellular damage, penetration point, or ring fracture. Nothing."

"Sounds like a case for Unsolved Mysteries, don't you think, Em?" Matt joked, trying to lighten the mood.

"It looks like the tree just grew right through it," the technician said, ignoring Matt's comment.

"The tree grew through a solid gold pen? Is that what you're saying?" Matt questioned, taking a closer look at the X-ray.

"But we all know that's impossible," the technician acknowledged, "The pen is inside the wood, though. Want me to cut it open? You need your pen back?"

Inside the starkly lit morgue, a portly coroner was pushing Amy's body toward a drawer when Matt burst through the doors, badge held high, finger jabbing through the air.

"Don't move that body," he commanded, echoing through the sterile space.

Quickly, he snatched up Amy's autopsy report, scanning it closely and flipping through the pages. "I don't see anything in here about her being pregnant," he stated, his eyes never leaving the document.

"She's not," replied the coroner, exasperation evident in his voice.

"You checked?" Matt persisted, finally looking up from the report.

The coroner nodded. Glancing at the clock, he noted it was already past 5:00 p.m. He moved to roll Amy's body away again, but Matt stopped him.

"You're absolutely sure?" Matt insisted, tension in his voice.

"Look, same as the others. What is this, some kind of game?" the coroner complained. "I got a crematorium burning one minute and fifteen seconds overtime. We signed the death certificate at 3:57 p.m. exactly. So, how long do you think I've been doing my job? Thirty seconds or thirty years?"

In the hall outside the morgue, Matt confronted Emily. "False alarm. It looks like your source was wrong. She wasn't pregnant," he said, his voice filled with relief and annoyance.

"Reporters sometimes make better cops than some cops," Emily shot back, standing her ground.

"Sometimes good cops don't need to be told how to do their jobs," he retorted, his temper flaring.

"The best ones don't," she replied coolly, undeterred by his anger.

He pulled her aside, lowering his voice. "I don't know what the hell you and this kid are up to, but let me tell you something. You are treading in dangerous waters right now, impeding an investigation."

"Hmm," Emily retorted, shoving a scrap of paper into Matt's hand.

"I'm not checking this out," he protested, frustration clear in his voice.

"For the man who trusts no one and believes in nothing," Emily quipped, watching as he unfolded the note and read it. "Thick headed and resilient and thinks he can read minds."

In a spacious office lined with medical journals, awards, certificates, and a surprising array of golf trophies, Matt sat across an oak desk from Dr. Serena, a distinguished-looking OB-GYN of about fifty-five years.

"You look puzzled, detective. Is something wrong?" she began, peering at him over the rim of her glasses.

"I had no idea you were Amy Johnson's doctor. You have an excellent reputation," Matt replied, leaning back in his chair.

"Being an expert witness for the county does not preclude me from having a practice. How can I help you?" she asked, folding her hands on the desk.

"Amy Johnson passed away in her sleep," Matt stated bluntly.

"I'm sorry to hear that," Dr. Serena responded, her face a mask of professional concern.

"We're investigating the possibility of foul play," Matt continued.

"Who would do such a thing?" she wondered aloud, genuine shock marking her features.

"That's what I'm trying to find out," Matt said, mirroring her somber tone.

"Amy was a brilliant person, a dancer, amateur astronomer. She was studying law at Stanford, preparing for the Bar."

"Can you tell me anything about any current medical condition she might have had? Medication, chronic symptoms of any kind?"

Dr. Serena sighed, "It's privileged, but aside from an excellent medical history, the most obvious was that she was pregnant."

"Pregnant? You're sure of that?" Matt questioned, surprise coloring his tone.

"Second trimester. I'm very sure," she confirmed.

"Then the coroner would have seen that?" Matt asked, trying to connect the dots.

"Naturally. It should be in his report. After the miscarriage the last time, I knew she wanted a baby girl. This is awful news," Dr. Serena shared, a soft sadness filling her voice.

"Excuse me. The last time?" Matt asked, his confusion escalating.

"A few years back. Amy had all the signs of being pregnant.

She was in her second trimester. Then nothing. The fetus just vanished. No, this time, it was different. I have the ultrasound results if you'd care to see them?" Dr. Serena offered.

Matt was deeply disturbed, his mind reeling from the revelation.

5

Under the pallid glow of his office lamp, Matt studied the reports spread across his desk. His attention moved between the wooden block, two contradictory X-ray photos of Amy's uterus—one revealing a fetus, the other barren—and his assistant Zeppo's recent acquisitions: pizza, coffee, and batteries.

Zeppo was in high spirits, fascinated with a toy helicopter he'd picked up alongside the necessary items. "This really flies," he boasted, a childish twinkle in his eyes.

"Great. This doesn't. You get the lab report?" Matt asked, an air of impatience evident in his tone. As if to emphasize his seriousness, he jabbed his finger into the rotor blade of the miniature helicopter, causing it to crash onto the desk and fall apart.

"Cheap piece of shit," Zeppo muttered, trying to hide his disappointment as he gathered the scattered pieces.

"Preliminary says no bullets. She wasn't strangled. No poison. No drugs. Nothing," Zeppo reported, glancing at his disassembled toy. "Now, can I fly?"

"They checked everything in her blood? CBC panel?" Matt pressed, flipping through the pages of a black binder.

"Twice. Want to hear this? The cause of death on the coroner's report was natural expiration. Sounds like a license plate, don't it?" Zeppo joked, reaching for his toy helicopter.

"You mean natural causes."

"Whatever."

"We got nothing. Again," Matt lamented, feeling the weight of their fruitless efforts.

"Personally, I think it was one of two things: a pro hit or the clam sauce and red wine. The two just don't mix," Zeppo theorized, starting to reassemble his toy.

"Twenty-three-year-olds don't just die in their sleep," Matt retorted, refusing to accept Zeppo's simplistic conclusions.

Zeppo took a final look at the evidence, then focused on his toy helicopter, but not before sharing one more theory. "She had an abortion. She didn't tell her boyfriend. Probably didn't want the old man to know either. What an embarrassment that would be!"

"Why do you say that?" Matt asked, intrigued despite himself.

"Because of the family. The old duffer's a federal judge. Very pro-life," Zeppo explained, replacing the batteries in his toy.

"How very?" Matt probed further.

"Very, very. Roe v. Wade stuff. Heavy. He would look like a hypocrite if word got out. If I were his daughter humping this left-wing dip, I woulda' had heart failure too," Zeppo responded with a cynical chuckle. He picked up the block of wood encased in a plastic evidence bag. "And this little handy-dandy? What's this?"

"There's a pen inside," Matt informed him.

"Really?" Zeppo pretended to write with it, not missing a beat, before noticing the X-ray that revealed the pen embedded within the woodcut. "Very nice. How'd you get the pen inside there?"

"It grew," Matt replied dryly.

"Now I know where to look whenever we need a pen," Zeppo quipped, still examining the X-ray.

Their banter was interrupted by the arrival of a mailroom messenger who dropped off a stack of inter-office mail. As Matt thumbed through it, he located a police artist's rendering of the killer—a featureless, bald Asian man with huge dark eyes—and passed it to Zeppo.

"Do you know this guy?" he asked his assistant, who took a long, hard look at the thin-lipped stranger with no ears and shook his head.

"Scary. Sometimes I ask myself why I'm a cop," Zeppo admitted, breaking their silence.

"And?" Matt prompted, curious about Zeppo's contemplation.

"Hey, I never said I had the answer. I just ask the question," Zeppo responded with a nonchalant shrug. His eyes then wandered to an envelope from Emily.

"Just like old times. Oh, but none of that lilac scent that used to drive me wild," he teased, earning an unamused glare from Matt.

Once opened, the envelope revealed a handwritten note from Emily. After reading it, Matt passed it to Zeppo.

"An implant in the Corpus callosum? Jesus, she must be reading her own shit. How could she know this stuff?" Zeppo exclaimed, both impressed and bewildered.

"That's what I'm going to find out," Matt affirmed, his gaze again falling on the assortment of reports and photographs. Meanwhile, Zeppo focused on the tiny chopper perched atop the mysterious woodblock.

"Listen, I think I can market this. Get us a new career. What do you think? Best chopper on the block!" he proposed, unable to resist one last playful comment before the night claimed them.

Bathed in the soft glow of the moonlight, the detective pulled up to Emily's secluded cabin. He exited his vehicle and approached, rapping gently on the door. After a brief moment, the door creaked open to reveal Emily dressed down for the night and looking beguiling despite the late hour.

"Isn't it a little late to be working, detective? Or is it true what they say, the best cops never sleep?" Emily queried, her voice layered with a mix of sarcasm and exhaustion.

"May I come in?" he asked, avoiding her question.

"It's late, Matt. Please!" Emily replied, crossing her arms and blocking the doorway, a clear sign of her reluctance to let him in.

The tension in the air was thick as he struggled to voice the apology that had been building up inside him for so long. "Look, I'm sorry," he blurted out, breaking the silence.

She was taken aback. A stunned expression briefly flashed across her face. "I'm sorry for what happened before. I was in over my head. I made a mistake," he added, hoping to thaw the ice that had formed between them.

"No, you just blocked out anything you didn't want to hear," Emily retorted, her words sharp as a blade.

"I didn't mean to. It's just how I am," he admitted, revealing a level of vulnerability he rarely showed.

"It doesn't matter now," Emily replied curtly, beginning to shut the door on him.

"I need you to forget about what happened. I've changed," he pleaded, resisting her attempts to close the door.

"Matt, I don't know if I can ever forgive you. What you did really hurt. But I guess you had your reasons, right?" she spoke, her voice laced with hurt, before slamming the door in his face.

"Emily, please. I know I can't fix the past. I want to, but I don't know what to do," he called out to the closed door. He shuffled back to his car, starting a self-deprecating monologue.

"I was a creep. I was an idiot. Why am I saying this? I don't know. Look, this is confusing," he mumbled, meandering aimlessly into the nearby woods.

"How would I know I would have these feelings? I'm just a man. It's okay, it's okay. I come out here. I turn into a nervous wreck. I hate this. I can't function. I can't think straight. It's just, uh... well, I'm sort of a left-brained animal, jerk, creep, asshole. But what could I do about it, God? Nothing. You made me this way," he spoke into the abyss, his frustration reaching a boiling point.

Back at the cabin, the door creaked open again. Emily bathed in the soft light from inside and walked towards him, her hands tucked behind her back.

"What could I do?" he yelled, echoing through the silent woods.

"You could have been more of a man and less of a cop, Matt," she spoke, her words slicing through the cool night air like a dagger.

His gaze locked on her as she moved steadily towards him. The moonlight reflected in her eyes and off the object she held.

"You could have had a little respect for me. I never would have done that to you or anyone," she accused him, her voice echoing through the quiet night.

As she lifted her arm, he caught sight of the baseball bat she had been holding behind her back. He stumbled back in surprise, fear reflected in his eyes.

"Look, I wanted it to end. It was the only way I knew how. I'm sorry," he stammered, desperately trying to justify his actions.

Suddenly, she swung the bat. It collided with a tree with a resonating crack, and Matt fell onto his back in shock.

Emily looked down at him, lying on the ground.

"What always bothered me was that you had to let me find it out. You didn't have the guts to say what you felt," she accused him, her words biting through the calm of the night.

"I didn't know how I felt," Matt defended, trying to explain his actions and the mess they had created.

"You couldn't even tell me. Why, Matt? Was I so bad? Did you hate me that much?" Emily shot back, her voice laden with hurt and anger. She swung the bat against the tree, snapping a branch.

"Emily, I'm sorry. I didn't know any other way," Matt confessed, sliding down into a dry creek bed, distancing himself from her wrath.

"I didn't do anything wrong. You know that. I loved you. We had something special, and you ruined it. You can never make that up to me now," Emily accused, her voice breaking slightly.

Matt lost his footing in the dark and slipped into a running stream.

"Emily, I never wanted to hurt you, believe me. I just wasn't ready. I'm sorry. I really am sorry for both of us," Matt pleaded, his voice barely above a whisper.

She took a deep breath, lowering the bat that had until a moment ago, seemed so threatening. "This is the saddest, most dangerous day of my life," she declared quietly.

6

Hesitantly, soaking wet, Matt reached out a hand towards her. She mirrored his action, their hands meeting in the space between them. They leaned into each other, their lips meeting in a passionate kiss, falling to the ground, Emily laid her head on his shoulder and draped an arm around his waist, her gaze drifting upwards to the stars overhead.

Looking up, her eyes found solace in the inky black expanse of the night sky, dotted with a million twinkling stars. His hand found its way to her back, their bodies swaying slightly to the rhythm of the gentle breeze that whistled through the evergreens in the canyon.

His hand reached out, wavering slightly in the dim light, and she reciprocated, moving closer until their lips met. It was a passionate kiss that saw them sinking to their knees, toppling onto the ground.

With a soft tug, she took his hand and led him back inside.

"You need a towel."

Matt stood and took her hand, and she led him back inside the cabin.

.   .   .

Inside the intimacy of her bedroom that night, they made love. Their movements were gentle, their touches careful, and their whispers tender. The rest of the world fell away as they explored each other, leaving only the two in the soft glow of their shared passion.

The oil lamps within the cabin emitted a warm, cozy glow, and romantic music added to the ambiance.

They rose early in the morning to the sound of crows in the distance.

"You want coffee?" Emily asked, breaking the silence.

"Water's fine," Matt replied.

"Tap, okay?"

He nodded.

Emily returned with a glass of iced water for him and a cup of tea for herself. They stood at the counter, Matt holding up the note he had found.

"I got this. You want to tell me what you saw?" he asked, curiosity lacing his words.

After a short pause, Emily glanced at the note and said, "Amy was a really decent person, Matt," her tone was sincere.

"I'm sure she was," Matt replied, equally earnest in his agreement.

"Last Thanksgiving, her father was going to pay to fly her home. Instead, she passed out turkey and hot soup at the Mission in San Francisco," Emily recalled, her eyes holding a distant memory.

"I didn't know that," Matt confessed, his brows furrowing slightly.

"Down by the old pier, in the rocks, there's a colony of abandoned cats. Baby kittens that grow up in the wild. Sleep in the cold. Every morning before class, Amy would go there and feed them. She took time off to care for them when they were sick," Emily continued, the reverence for her neighbor evident in her voice.

"Nobody would do that," Matt said, a hint of awe entering his voice.

Emily pulled herself together, forcing her sorrow away. "Why did this have to happen to her? Who could have been so menacing, so hateful?" she wondered aloud, her voice breaking toward the end.

Matt held out the note she had left about the implant in the forebrain. "What about this?" he questioned, his gaze locked on her.

Emily started to search for a tissue. Sensing her need, Matt stood and handed her his handkerchief. She accepted it with a grateful nod.

"Josh told me," she disclosed, her voice muffled slightly.

"Why didn't he say something before?" Matt probed, his curiosity piqued.

"I had to drag it out of him," Emily admitted, a grimace crossing her face.

"How did it get there?" Matt asked, staring at her expectantly.

"Maybe we should sit down," Emily suggested, her expression serious.

"Why?" Matt queried, his eyebrows knitting together in confusion.

"Because I have a feeling you're not going to like what I'm about to say," Emily warned, her eyes locked onto his.

Heeding her suggestion, Matt perched himself on the edge of the sofa. Emily took a deep breath, readying herself for the revelation.

"Who implanted it?" Matt asked, his voice edged with anticipation.

"Little gray men," Emily declared, her voice steady.

Matt stared at her in disbelief. "You mean dwarfs in costumes?" he asked, trying to make sense of her statement.

"No, Matt. The reason Josh couldn't remember what happened wasn't that he didn't want to. It was because he was under a post-hypnotic suggestion," Emily revealed, her gaze unwavering.

"By who?" Matt asked, now even more curious and unsettled than before.

"I just told you," Emily stated, her voice steady despite the incredulousness of her revelation.

"You're saying little gray men placed an implant into Amy Johnson's skull, and Josh was hypnotized while this whole thing was going on?" Matt asked disbelief, coloring his words.

"Yes, that's how it works," Emily confirmed, meeting his gaze unflinchingly.

"Incredible," Matt breathed, rising from the sofa. He paced the room, struggling to process what he was hearing.

"It gets worse. I took Josh to a hypnotist, the same one the police use in really tough cases," Emily divulged, her voice dropping slightly.

"And?" Matt prompted, pausing in his pacing to turn and look at her.

"He started remembering things. The things he talked about are similar to screen images other alien abductees have expressed. There's been a significant flap period in recent years. I didn't want to reinvent the wheel. So, she regressed him," Emily explained, her tone impassive.

"And under hypnosis, Josh was able to recall the events about these little gray men?" Matt queried, his disbelief still lingering.

"Most of them," Emily replied, nodding slightly.

"Look, I can't do anything with this. I'd be laughed out of the department," Matt admitted, his frustration bubbling to the surface.

"Matt, something happened that night. Something very strange," Emily insisted, a particular determination lining her voice.

"I'll say. I've got a serial killer out there who murders young women in their sleep and leaves no tracks," Matt retorted, his voice laden with stress.

"Josh experienced something that scared him so much he couldn't talk about it. He couldn't even remember," Emily said, her voice softening.

"I'm listening. But this is not easy for me," Matt confessed, his eyes reflecting his inner turmoil.

"Imagine something happening to you, something so terrifying and so wrong that they would have Amy killed? Whatever she saw, they wanted to make sure no one ever found out," Emily proposed, her voice strained.

"Found out what?" Matt asked, breaking from his spot to get up and pacing again.

"We are not dealing with your average psychopath, Matt. We are dealing with your average psychopathic killer alien. And you can't do anything about it," Emily asserted, her voice carrying a note of finality. She tossed a couple of exterior photos on the table. A strange series of lights floated over the cabin. Matt paused in his pacing to examine the images. "Images from the security camera."

With a determined look, Emily turned on a tape recorder and hit the play button. Josh's voice filled the room.

"They're coming in. I see them. They're here."

A moment of silence followed before another voice, presumably the hypnotist's Dr. Medea's, echoed in the room. "Who, Josh, who are they?"

"They're small, gray. Floating. No, no. Amy... No!" Josh's

voice panted through the speakers, his tone escalating into a panic. The tape played on, ending eventually with Josh's terrifying scream.

7

Matt sat there, his eyes wide with astoundment, unable to form a coherent thought. By the end of the conversation, Matt was left with an eerie sense of unease, wondering if they were dealing with an average psychopathic killer or something far more alien. Emily's evidence, the photos of strange lights, and Josh's panicked voice on tape only deepened his apprehension.

"Your mouth is open," Emily commented, a hint of dry amusement in her voice.

Matt stood up, pacing the room as if the physical activity could help him digest the outlandish revelation. He ran a hand through his hair, a gesture of bewildered frustration.

"That's one hell of a story, Emily," he finally said, his voice thick with disbelief.

Emily glanced at his empty water glass. "Something stronger?" she suggested, rising from her seat.

Pouring a couple of glasses of Glenfiddich, she handed one to Matt, who gratefully accepted it. He downed the amber liquid, his face scrunching momentarily at the burn.

"Bizarre," he muttered, setting the empty glass back on the table.

"Life is bizarre," Emily retorted, her expression serious.

"Emily, come on. Little green men?" Matt asked, a skeptical grin spreading across his face.

"Gray, Matt. They were gray EBEs, extraterrestrial biological entities," Emily corrected, her tone matter-of-fact.

"This isn't police work. This is what you read about at the supermarket checkout line," Matt argued, waving a dismissive hand.

"Exactly," Emily agreed, her voice calm.

"You don't need a detective. You need a psychic. This is fantasy," Matt stated, his voice carrying a tone of finality.

"Amy is dead. Is that fantasy, too?" Emily countered, her voice rising slightly.

"She died of a heart attack. That's all. Case closed," Matt declared, establishing the boundary between the plausible and the ridiculous.

"You're a cop, Matt. There's been a murder," Emily insisted, unwilling to let go of her belief in the extraordinary circumstances surrounding Amy's death.

"This was no murder. There was no weapon," Matt protested, shaking his head.

"The implant," Emily reminded, her voice almost a whisper.

"What implant?" Matt queried, looking genuinely confused.

"In her brain," Emily clarified, staring him down.

"There's no motive," Matt argued, throwing up his hands in frustration.

"Yet," Emily retorted, her voice stern.

"No suspect," Matt added, his voice tinged with resignation.

"It's your job to find this guy and bring him to justice," Emily declared, her gaze unwavering.

"I've got no case. I'm going to charge a fucking alien from

outer space with murder?" Matt scoffed, the ridiculousness of the idea striking him hard.

"Yes," Emily said, her voice firm.

Matt's response was a burst of laughter, bitter and skeptical.

"You've got a case, and you damn well know it. You're just too scared to look, too afraid to face the truth about these abductions. You're as terrified as everybody else that you'll end up on the cover of my magazine," Emily accused, her words dripping with anger and frustration.

"Oh, you got that right," Matt retorted, a self-deprecating smirk curving his lips.

"This is happening all over the world, Matt, and no one is paying any attention to it. People and kids are disappearing every day, and no one knows what the hell is going on. It's your job to find out and put an end to it if you're man enough," Emily countered, her voice echoing through the room, the words heavy with desperation.

"So, where would you suggest I start looking for this guy? The DMV? See if they got a make on his little spaceship or at least the license plate?"

"That would help."

"Or maybe I should turn it over to the Air Force? Maybe they know something we don't?" Matt joked, his sarcasm as dry as sandpaper.

"They closed the case on Project Blue Book in 1970. Officially, there are no UFOs," Emily answered, her voice devoid of emotion.

Deciding that he'd had enough, Matt got up and strode towards the door. "There's nothing I can do," he stated, his back to her.

"Matt, please just take one more look. That's all I'm asking. And if there's nothing here, I'll drop the whole thing, and maybe we can mend some fences," Emily pleaded, her voice softer now, filled with a specific uncharacteristic vulnerability.

He opened the door, his hand lingering on the knob. He turned back to face her, his eyes searching hers. "Let me ask you something. Why are you so gung-ho about this?" he inquired, curiosity painting his features.

"When the forensic team finds the implant, could you just call me?" Emily requested, her gaze never leaving his.

8

───────

In the cold, sterile environment of the morgue, Dr. Roger Leir, surgeon and ufologist, was invited to work meticulously to extract a tiny silver implant, barely three millimeters long, from the right nostril of the deceased woman, Amy Johnson. The tiny object resembled a minute silver pin, its purpose mystifying.

"I don't like opening old cases, and I just don't see how you could have overlooked this," Matt told the coroner.

"It didn't show up on the X-rays. What is it?" the coroner asked, his tone tinged with confusion.

Looking at the foreign object, Matt quipped, "A thermometer."

Dr. Leir deposited the tiny device onto a specimen tray as a medical technician stood by. Swiftly, Matt scooped it up, delicately placing it within the folds of a pristine white handkerchief before sealing it in an evidence bag.

"Any sign of concussion or head wounds like she might have hit a wall?" Leir queried, his mind already churning through the implications.

"Negative. We checked," the coroner responded, leaving no room for doubt.

Matt probed further into Amy's physical state, seeking confirmation about pregnancy, abortion, and rape. Still, the coroner reassured him that there were no such indications. Surprisingly, the only anomalies were two tiny scoop marks at the base of her spine.

"Except for these two tiny little birthmarks, she's as clean as a whistle. In fact, she was just beginning to ovulate. Right on schedule. Like clockwork," the coroner said, his years of experience evident in his matter-of-fact tone.

A young technical wizard examined the curious pine core at an independent forensic lab. Matt looked on as he used various sophisticated devices, his nimble fingers and quick eyes doing a thorough examination.

"Like the ship in the bottle, huh? You always wonder how these alloys got in there," the young tech mused, comparing them to their present predicament.

"I stopped wondering long ago," Matt replied, his tone a bit weary.

The tech continued his analysis, stating that whoever inserted the device knew what they were doing and that the technique was highly advanced. "Whoever got it in here did a hell of a job."

"Which means?"

"They really knew what they were doing," the tech continued.

"Why?" asked Matt.

"Think of this like water instead of wood, okay? Then, pretend the pen is like a tube of Jell-O. The Jell-O is in the water. It gets a little wet. But in the water, no Jell-O. The Jell-O is semi-permeable, let's say. So, some gets through. But that's not happening, right? Because this is wood and not water, and that's a pen and not Jell-O."

However, his analogy of the core acting like water and the device akin to a tube of Jell-O seemed more philosophical than scientific to Matt.

"Very Zen. What about the implant?"

After using X-ray diffraction, the tech retrieved the implant from a scanner, and his computer screen drew a blank.

"Negative on the patent search. No functioning parts. Light, tough. Strange alloy. Trace elements of tellurium, cadmium, and carbon. Maybe Uup, element 115. I'd have to run more tests," he said.

He held it up with tweezers and applied a blowtorch to no effect. His astounding conclusion: "I'd say you got yourself a secret weapon here, Chief. It reads like they manufactured it on the moon."

Matt's reply was flippant: "Not Mars?"

But the tech held firm, indicating the specific gravity and ionization were incorrect for Mars, suggesting it might be a space station experiment.

"Well, whatever it is, it's flawless. It was not created by human hands," he added, his words striking a note of finality.

He dropped the tiny silver implant into Matt's waiting handkerchief using his gloved hand. Matt rolled it up and placed it in the evidence bag, a shiver of foreboding going down his spine.

As Matt navigated through the labyrinth of glass cubicles at the police station, he spotted a group of men clad in dark suits, engaged in hushed discussions with the Chief of Police. He synced up with Zeppo, his partner on the force.

"Big pow-wow," Zeppo muttered, his eyes trained on the gathering.

"Who's the old guy with the feds?" Matt asked, his gaze catching an unfamiliar face among the law enforcement officials.

"That's the girl's father, the judge. Blew a fuse when he found out," Zeppo replied, the concern evident in his voice.

The Police Chief, Judge Johnson, and two FBI agents were engrossed in a heated discussion. The tension in the room was palpable.

"What does he know?" Matt asked, his eyes never leaving the group.

"He ain't buying that natural causes bit, I can tell you that," Zeppo said, sympathetic in his tone.

"Maybe I should just go in and tell them about the little gray men," Matt suggested half in jest.

Zeppo snorted, "Is that your new theory?"

"It's one option," Matt replied, a trace of a smirk on his face.

Zeppo said, "Oh, I think they'd like that very much."

Matt glanced at the group again, noticing they were wrapping up their discussion. The Chief, typically the epitome of calm control, looked unusually strained as he approached Matt and Zeppo.

"Steel, Zeppo. We need to talk," the Chief said, his voice low and rumbling.

"I think we might have a breakthrough with these murders, Chief," Matt began, but the Chief cut him off.

"The Johnson case is closed, okay? So, file your reports," the Chief commanded.

"But, sir, forensic evidence points to new facts that would tie them together. All twelve murders," Matt insisted, his voice determined.

"Whatever evidence you've got will be sealed and filed, detective. That's an order," the Chief said dismissively.

Matt was not dissuaded. "Tom, I think there's more to this

case that you should know about. If you'd just give me a minute to explain," he said.

The Chief sighed, a rare crack in his usually stoic demeanor. "Look, Steel, the judge isn't about to sit still because his daughter may have been a victim of foul play. So, if I were you, I wouldn't pursue this case any further. The DA has closed the case. And we have too. Understood? It was a natural death. Heart arrhythmia."

As the Chief started to walk away, Matt grabbed his arm, prompting a look of disapproval from the Chief. "Tom, I've got a body. I've got a murder weapon. I've got a motive."

"But no suspects, right?" the Chief retorted, his patience wearing thin.

Matt didn't back down. "Not yet, but we're close."

The Chief scoffed. "Close? That's not the kind of police work we do here, Lieutenant."

"We have hard evidence," Matt retorted, his voice steady.

The Chief gestured towards the men in his office. "They are not interested."

"The facts in this case are all wrong," Matt protested, his frustration seeping into his words.

The FBI agents turned to scrutinize Matt, their sharp eyes making it clear that they would keep a close watch on him. Seeing this, Matt backed off. He had fought hard, but he knew when he was beaten.

"Whatever you have, turn it over," the Chief demanded, his tone final.

In the silence of an independent forensic lab, two men cloaked in black suits combed through the sterile environment, their sights set on the elusive implant. However, despite their thorough search, their efforts bore no fruit; the tiny piece of evidence remained hidden.

9

Hundreds of miles away in Dulce, New Mexico, a hulking figure marched down a stark, concrete-walled corridor. General Breakwater, a seasoned commander in his mid-sixties, was flanked by a cohort of American and Russian military police. Their grim faces mirrored the severity of their mission. With determined strides, the general burst into a conference room, his armed escort remaining at the door.

The room was shrouded in obscurity, its corners veiled in shadow. At the far end of the conference table sat an imposing figure, an Alien Commander. Compact yet robust, the alien was the leader of his kind, an outlandish presence in the human world. General Breakwater proceeded to the table, his face a hardened mask of resolve.

"You got me hopping mad, son," the general began, his voice echoing in the gloomy space. "It's one thing to fool with the boys upstairs, but this report is full of crap." He slammed a thick report onto the table, the sound reverberating ominously.

The general made out the creature's defining features from the scant light available. Large black insect-like eyes dominated a long, hairless head devoid of ears. A narrow chin met a sloping, featureless face, while a pocket-sized triangular crest adorned its chest. The alien possessed thin, unmoving lips, and an eerie, condescending benevolence colored its tone. Two alien escorts, similar in appearance, stood watchfully at its side.

"The report is correct," the Alien Commander communicated telepathically. The voice, hollow and distant, seemed to emanate from behind the general. Breakwater glanced behind him, unease settling in his features.

"Now we told you we'd do your guide work for you, but we're not handling your PR," the general retorted, his frustration evident.

"No one expects you to," the alien responded calmly.

Breakwater, however, was far from placated. He delivered an ultimatum, "You got a lying crew of Saturday night fly-boys hot-rodding around the country, and I want it to stop. Now!"

"I will look into it," the commander promised.

"Better look fast 'cause I ain't taking heat for your mistakes," Breakwater shot back, his anger flaring.

"There are no mistakes," the alien retorted defiantly.

Breakwater pointed accusingly at the report. "Then how do you explain this? A judge's daughter gets picked up and tagged, and she's not on the list? You're under-reporting your missions, commander. And that's not part of our arrangement."

"Do not call me a liar," the alien responded, the telepathic voice chilling in its resolute delivery.

Breakwater, undeterred, continued, "Let me make something perfectly clear to you. It's one thing to pick up a Hoosier from some cornfield in Indiana. It's a whole other bag 'o trouble to nip a blue blood in her prime. Folks don't like it, and they won't put up with it. You get the message?"

"You can leave now," the alien dismissed him coolly.

The general retreated, leaving the dimly lit room to its alien occupants. The door closed behind him, but not before a flurry of strange dialogue—sounding like rapid clicks played back-ward—resounded through the corridor.

Back in the corridor, Breakwater straightened his tie. The military police snapped to attention. The general grumbled under his breath, "Goddamn aliens think they own the fucking place." His frustration reverberated through the stark, cold hall-way, the echo a grim reminder of the complex situation they found themselves in.

10

The city's lights shimmered outside the grand windows of the Westwood hotel lobby. Not stopping to acknowledge the concierge, Matt swiftly entered the ornate archway into the lounge

A gentle tune echoed from a harp, filling the oak-paneled drawing room with a soothing melody. Scattered around, a few couples, students, and hotel guests lounged on antique sofas, their cocktails resting on the polished surfaces of rosewood end tables.

Matt approached a figure immersed in the music and art-adorned walls – Judge Johnson's silver hair contrasting sharply against the dark wood paneling. They'd crossed paths earlier at the police station.

"Judge Johnson, I'm Lieutenant Steel. Homicide LAPD," Matt introduced himself, interrupting the judge's musings.

"I'm glad you could see me on such short notice, Lieutenant. Tell me, what do you know about this case? About my daughter?" the judge inquired, his grip tight on his second scotch.

"It's a lot like the others," Matt replied a hint of somberness in his voice.

"The others?" the judge echoed, the question hanging heavy in the air.

"It seems your daughter was the thirteenth victim in a pattern of sudden unexplained deaths, sir. All twelve victims were young women between the ages of eighteen and twenty-seven. They all died in their sleep of some unknown cause. All were pregnant. They mysteriously miscarried. No weapons, no evidence, no real clues until now."

The judge's face paled. "You ever lose someone you love, Lieutenant?"

"Once," Matt responded, his gaze lowering slightly.

The judge's voice softened, a hint of melancholy tinging his words. "My wife passed away a few years back. Amy was our only child. I was determined to spend more time with her, but with the demands of the bench. You know how that goes. The Lord can't give those years back to you, can he?"

"No, sir, I don't suppose he can," Matt agreed, the shared sentiment of loss hanging between them.

In an unexpected move, Judge Johnson reached out to touch Matt's arm, glancing around the room to ensure their privacy. "Something is happening here that even a federal judge can't find out."

"The death certificate indicated an aneurysm. Circle of Willis in the anterior cerebral artery," Matt offered.

"What caused the aneurysm, Detective? Amy's grandfather is ninety-six. Her grandmother is ninety-seven. She was healthy and honest, too. She had that going for her, unlike these government spies and liars. We should throw the whole damn bunch out. How do you inspire children with ethics and values today when the world feeds on cover-ups and corruption?" the Johnson mused, finishing his drink.

"I don't want to change the subject, sir, but did Amy ever mention her dreams?" Matt ventured.

"A hardened detective like you, interested in dreams?" the judge chuckled.

"A lot of well-known people have paid attention to their dreams. Sometimes, it's saved their lives," said Matt.

"Well, let me think. When Amy was a little girl, she had dreams. I suppose you might call them nightmares," the judge revealed, looking into the distance as if the memories were playing out before him.

"How old was she?" Matt pressed.

"Seven, maybe eight."

"What happened?"

"Her mother and I were concerned about these apparitions."

"She saw things?"

"Invisible friends, but she saw them long after most kids stopped. So, we took Amy to a child psychologist."

"And?"

"There was one recurring nightmare, I remember," the judge admitted, his voice barely a whisper.

"Are you suggesting these apparitions were real?"

"Real enough to her. You see, Amy would tell us she was in some operating room, and there were insects, no, maybe owls, big bug-eyed owls crawling all over her. Imagine a little girl having that kind of imagination?" Johnson confessed, his gaze meeting Matt's.

A cold shiver ran down Matt's spine. As he looked away from the judge, two men dressed in black entered his peripheral vision, their watchful eyes firmly set on them.

"Go on," Matt urged, intrigued by the unusual account.

"These insects or owls or whatever were wearing doctor's gowns, and they'd give her a little doll and let her play with it for a while. And they'd take it away just when she had the hair fixed nicely and the little dress right. Then they'd give her another one and take that away," the judge elaborated, his eyes distant as he relived his daughter's strange tales.

"What did the shrink say?" Matt asked, trying to make sense of it all.

"A transitional dream, he called it. Giving up the things she knew as a child, letting go, and not being afraid. I guess we all have to face that kind of thing sometime, don't we?" Johnson pondered, his voice trailing off in thought.

"Yeah. Like letting go of the past and what we once were?" Matt added, a note of empathy in his tone.

"The world is changing, Detective. Fast. You know, there's someone I think you should meet. He was a friend of Senator Exon. I want you to talk to him. He knows people. I want you to find out what happened to my little girl," the judge finished with a desperate determination in his voice. He looked Matt squarely in the eyes, placing his faith in the Detective to unveil the truth behind his daughter's untimely demise.

11

———————

The metallic rasp of the key unlocking the door echoed in the dark confines of Matt's cluttered studio apartment. Shrugging off his leather jacket, he set his shoulder harness and gun, a Smith & Wesson 5906 semi-automatic 9 mm, on the bed, the sleek black metal gleaming under the faint light. His gaze fell on the evidence bags - one held the odd implant, the other the woodblock. A battalion of ants drew his attention as he lay on the bed. With a disgruntled sigh, he grabbed a can of Raid from the bedside table and sprayed the tiny invaders.

Above a cluttered bookshelf sat a worn baseball mitt, which he donned. He sent a hardball into its seasoned grip a few times. He fetched a cold Coors from the fridge before heading to the bathroom.

As he turned on the shower, Matt stripped down to his shorts, pounding the ball rhythmically into his glove as he waited for the water to heat up. The bathroom was an odd homage to his love for baseball, and the cards of famous players - Mickey Mantle, Ty Cobb, and the Babe - were taped to the mirror and wall. Written affirmations sprawled across the top of the medicine cabinet: "I Am A Good Cop," "A Good Cop Always Gets His Man," "Good Cops Hit Home Runs."

From the corner of his eye, Matt saw his front door reflected in the mirror. He slowly turned the mirror to follow the movement. A hitman, complete with a silencer, cautiously entered the apartment. His eyes were instantly drawn to the bed where the evidence bags lay. An immediate sense of alarm surged through Matt as he desperately scanned the bathroom for a potential weapon.

As the intruder moved closer to the evidence, Matt launched into a god-awful song rendition, watching the intruder from the corner of his eye. The distraction worked - the intruder froze, looking around the room as Matt lobbed his glove across the room. Startled, the hitman whirled around, firing a round from his silenced pistol.

Seizing his chance, Matt threw the baseball at the hitman's head, the impact causing the man to drop the implant. He tackled the thug, wrestling him for control of the gun. But the fight quickly turned chaotic as a second intruder entered the apartment, bullets flying as a third hitman appeared from the balcony. The room was a whirlwind of crossfire and adrenaline. Amidst the chaos, Matt scrambled for his 5906 semi-automatic. His hand brushed the can of Raid, tempting him with an unorthodox weapon.

His agility surprised even himself. Matt rolled, snatched the first hitman's silencer, fired at the second intruder at the door, and wounded the third, attempting to escape to the fire escape. Clutching the gun in one hand and the can of Raid in the other, he gave chase. But by the time he emerged onto the balcony, the third hitman had disappeared into the night.

·　·　·

Later, he confronted Emily in her living room at the cabin with a troubled look as he held up the tiny implant. "I hate bugs. You want to tell me what the hell is going on?"

"Why ask me?" Emily retorted, a tinge of exasperation in her voice.

"Because you were the one who told me about this scum," Matt shot back.

"You were investigating this case on your own," Emily countered.

"What about this?" Matt held up the implant.

"Oh, Matt, get rid of it. It should be in the evidence locker," Emily advised.

"Why?" Matt asked, his eyebrows furrowing in confusion.

"It's a cross between a homing beacon and a walkie-talkie. That's why," Emily

explained.

"Well, someone wanted this walkie-talkie pretty badly tonight. Maybe the parts weren't available at Radio Shack?" Matt's tone was laced with sarcasm.

"Or maybe you got the last one?" Emily suggested.

"I doubt it," Matt replied, shaking his head.

"You have no idea what you're dealing with, do you?" Emily asked, an edge to her voice.

"All I know is a girl dies in her sleep, you tell me some weird story, and the DA drops the case faster than a quick fuck. Next thing I know, three guys think this is the most critical doo-dad in the world," Matt snapped back.

"They'll know you're here," Emily warned.

"Who?" Matt demanded, his patience wearing thin.

Under the inky cloak of the night, Matt navigated Emily's sleek black Corvette down a twisting road. The surrounding darkness was punctuated by the car's headlights cutting a narrow path through the obscurity.

"Just like old times," he remarked, glancing at Emily, who stared pensively out the window.

"With you in control?" Emily replied, her tone carrying a hint of mockery.

"Who says I'm in control?" Matt asked, a crooked smile playing on his lips.

"Oh, I know you're not," she said confidently.

"Who says I'm not?" He retorted, his smile broadening.

"You did. Where are you taking me?" Emily turned to face him, her brow furrowing in curiosity.

"You suggested a drive. Ever hear of John Lear?" Matt asked, his gaze fixed on the road ahead.

"As in Lear jet?" Emily asked, her interest piqued.

"His son. Ex-CIA pilot with lots of top speed records. Used to fly for Patriot. Canned a couple of years back. You know why?" Matt's voice was full of intrigue.

"We put him on the front page of our newspaper once," Emily recalled.

"That practically killed him," Matt commented, a sense of seriousness permeating his voice.

"Thanks. That was my Press Award for Front Page of the Year," Emily retorted, a tinge of annoyance in her voice.

"Seems Judge Johnson has a buddy in the Senate who spent some time looking at these things. The chair of the Senate Committee on Intelligence. He says Lear is a reliable source," Matt revealed as they continued their journey into the night.

12

A rattlesnake slithered up the stairs of a Las Vegas desert mobile home. Inside the drab room, the police composite of the alien loomed on the screen, filling the space with its eerie presence. It bore an uncanny resemblance to the extraterrestrial on the cover of the book, "Communion." The alien, with its large, dark, slanted eyes, triangular face devoid of ears, and thin nose, bore a disturbingly impassive expression.

John Lear, a handsome yet nervous man in his late fifties, scrutinized the alien drawing. "I know this guy," he admitted.

"From where?" Matt asked, leaning in slightly.

"You want to know if I still believe there's a UFO cover-up? That's why you came?" Lear queried, looking at Matt.

"Yeah," Matt answered without hesitation.

Lear paused, his gaze falling on the alien sketch again. "Detective, my feelings are the same as the senator. There has to be. If there wasn't, do you realize what would happen? This is a matter of national security."

Emily said, her fingers poised above a recorder app on her phone, "What about other EBEns? Have you ever seen any?"

"I saw E.T., But I've never seen him shopping at Safeway," Lear responded dryly.

"What about this guy?" Matt pointed at the police sketch, but Lear only shook his head.

"Even in a murder investigation, this is not something you should mess with. This whole subject is classified above top secret, even higher than the H-bomb."

"We need to find him. It's important. You helped Senator Exon once before," Matt pushed further.

"That's not exactly true. Look, this might help. But after this, you're on your own," Lear said, navigating through a cluttered shelf to locate a videocassette. He inserted it into the VCR and hit play.

The footage of a spaceship landing at Holloman Air Force Base in New Mexico in 1954 played out on-screen. Lear narrated, "This is the actual military footage. Is it real? Is it fake? Who knows? Who cares, right? The question you want to ask yourself is, if it is real, so what?"

Emily reacted, "So what? This is a major story."

"Also, a perilous one," Lear countered.

"You lost your job because you asked that question," Matt pointed out.

Lear nodded, "And almost my life, but all I'm saying now is you have to get beyond this two-stage thinking."

Emily interjected, "What do you mean?"

"Are there, aren't there, are there, aren't there? Who cares?" Lear dismissed.

"Somebody cares," Matt insisted.

Lear took a deep breath, "What's important is if they exist and we're hiding it, why?"

"National security," Matt offered.

"Security, sure. That's the cover story. Free energy, anti-gravity, and propulsion drives of their craft. We've reverse-engineered all their technology. Ben Rich hinted at that, but they're still ahead of us," Lear explained.

Suddenly, a slow-motion, black-and-white amateur film showing President Kennedy allegedly being shot by the Secret Service driver of his limousine, William Greer, in Dallas, 1963, played on the screen. Lear paused the tape and turned to his guests, "He was in favor of disclosure, but they couldn't let him tell the truth."

Emily asked, her voice just a whisper, "Who?"

Lear paused momentarily before speaking; his gaze transfixed on some unseen point. "MJ-12. Since the Roswell crash in 1947, Majestic Twelve has been the official secret group in charge of alien activities here on Earth. Everybody knows that."

"I didn't think they were real," Emily confessed, her brow furrowed in skepticism.

"Oh, MJ-12 is real, all right. Dr. Vannevar Bush, James Forrestal, Secretary of Defense, Vice Admiral Roscoe Hillenkoetter, Dr. Lloyd Berkner, Hoyt Vandenberg. The list goes on. They're real. They are dead, but they're still with us. Freedom of Information documents are getting released every day," Lear countered, his voice firm and confident.

"Why would they allow it? For what purpose?" Matt asked, attempting to understand the complexities of the situation.

"To acclimate us, to make us think these grays are friendly," Lear stated, his eyes still glued to the alien sketch.

"And they're not?" Matt asked, his voice a mix of curiosity and apprehension.

"These ones are fucking deadly," Lear replied grimly.

"Then there are others?" Matt asked, trying to keep pace with the stream of startling revelations.

"Yeah. Seems simple, doesn't it?" Lear responded with a shrug.

Emily sighed, "And you're mocked as a fool if you believe it."

"And a bigger fool if you don't," Lear added, a wry smile playing on his lips.

"Where would you suggest I find this guy?" Matt inquired, holding out the sketch of the gray.

"Matt, I don't know who you're really with, but I don't believe any of this stuff. None of us do. So, if you want me to help you find this guy, let me offer you one piece of advice. You don't find them. They find you," Lear explained, staring intently at the drawing of the visitor. He scribbled a name and city on a note and handed it to Matt. "Try Jason Bishop."

13

Emily checked her phone for GPS, but there was no signal. So she examined a street map sprawled across the hood of their parked car along an open highway in Sedona, Arizona. A striking, round, reddish landmass, the Bell Tower energy vortex, reached up to touch the cloudless blue sky. On the other hand, Matt was absorbed in the awe-inspiring view of the majestic landscape, preparing for their journey into the unknown.

Matt and Emily made their way to the front desk inside a sanatorium. A young desk clerk, a naive twenty-one-year-old with an air of New Age whimsy, greeted them with a quirky grin.

"Can I, like, help you?" she asked, her voice holding a sing-song lilt.

"Is this 1241 Greenlawn Lane?" Matt asked.

"If you want to call that lawn green," she retorted sarcastically.

"And Jason Bishop lives here?" Matt continued, unfazed.

"Well, if you call zzsstt... living," she answered cryptically, her eyes sparkling with amusement.

"Zzsst?" Matt queried, a look of bewilderment crossing his face.

With a pointed look, the clerk mimed a bolt of electricity coursing through her head and went, "Zzzsstt." Then, sizing them up, she fell silent.

"May we see him?" Emily interjected, trying to move the conversation forward.

"Is it his birthday or something? You're the second group today," the clerk remarked with surprise. "Look, I'm looped. The air stinks, the water is foul, and the world is about to end any day."

"We just need to talk to him for a few minutes. We won't breathe on him," Matt promised, a tinge of impatience coloring his words.

"He used to live here. But he got out," the clerk replied cryptically.

"Where did he go?" Matt asked, his interest piqued.

"Secret underground base," she replied as if it was the most obvious thing in the world.

"What?" Matt blinked in surprise.

"No. Not what, where?" she corrected him. "It's in the mountains, past the canyon. Lots of snakes. Everybody knows where it is."

"Why did he go there?" Emily questioned, struggling to keep up with the rapid-fire information.

"To finish his book, which is brilliant," the clerk gushed. "But then, he made a big mistake. He took it to APRO."

"APRO? The dog food company?" Matt inquired, thoroughly confused now.

"It should be," she giggled. "No. It's like the Aerial Phenomena Research Organization. What kind of name is that? Too many syllables. Anyway, they had Jason like committed to the New Mexico State Hospital. Cool place. When they fried enough brain cells, they shipped the mass of bizarro flesh back here."

"The base?" Matt guessed.

"Lloyd Butte," she clarified.

"Who's Lloyd Butte?" Matt asked, more confused than ever.

"Gawd, not who. Where," she groaned. "It's where Jason would go. A sacred Indian ruin on the other side of Boyington Canyon. To get his shit together. You need to go there. It will chill you out. Too intense."

"You think I need to chill?" Matt asked, raising an eyebrow.

"Definitely," she replied, handing him a tattered paperback titled 'THE DULCE REPORT' on secret underground UFO bases. "I've done the vortexes. I can read your mind. You're way too intense for this place. It'll help you talk to him."

"I think I can read your mind, too," Matt smirked. "Childhood gift."

The vast Boyington Canyon vortex towered above them, rising hundreds of feet. The rusty stronghold was intimidating and pockmarked with dark caves. It looked like an ancient seabed as if it had been submerged underwater millions of years ago. Matt parked their vehicle in a dusty clearing, and he and Emily stepped out, hiking through the desert scrub.

"I don't think I'm that intense," Matt remarked, squinting against the bright sun.

"You're calmer than a desert rat. Is your gun loaded?" Emily replied, her gaze scanning the surrounding area.

As they neared the rock fortress, the vegetation thickened around them. A rugged path led up to a broken set of stone steps. They carefully started their ascent.

"The Hopi Indians lived here a thousand years ago," Emily commented, focusing on the path ahead.

"What happened? Were they abducted, too?" Matt asked a tinge of sarcasm in his voice.

"Sure. All of them. Vanished, without a trace. The aliens ate them," Emily answered dryly.

Matt stopped, reading a highlighted section of Bishop's book. "A woman and her daughter saw aliens mutilate a calf in a field. Not farmers, not the military, Emily. Not ranchers, but little aliens. Then they were abducted too."

"Must have been lunchtime. Does he say where?" Emily queried a trace of amusement in her tone.

"Where else? The underground base diner." Matt rolled his eyes.

"They get out?" Emily asked, trying to keep the conversation focused.

"Must have, right before dessert. They told their story to Bishop. The poor lady claims she saw body parts floating in amber fluid. She was probably farsighted and staring at a dirty toilet after a hard night out," Matt said sarcastically.

"Matt," Emily warned.

"Bishop writes this stuff as though it was fact, Emily. It's all hearsay. He's got nothing to back it up," Matt countered, frustration in his voice.

"He was a respected scientist before this happened. He was forced to use an alias," Emily defended.

"Because he went over the edge," Matt shot back.

"He found aliens, Matt. Just like the ones who killed Amy," Emily countered, her voice steady.

"I don't see how Lear could ever believe this guy. No one else saw this base. Nothing could be confirmed. No vet's post-examination of any cattle. Nothing," Matt argued, his patience waning.

"Exactly. It's perfect," Emily said, her tone matter-of-fact.

"Emily, local ranchers deny ever missing any cattle," Matt pointed out.

"They were afraid to talk," Emily insisted.

"Why?" Matt questioned, his brow furrowing.

"Piece it together. Bishop, or whoever he was, was on the inside. A distinguished government research scientist. He was right in the middle of this thing. His only way out was to go public. A whistleblower," Emily explained.

"What if we find out he made it all up?" Matt asked, his eyes clouded with skepticism.

"You think Amy Johnson made it up?" Emily challenged him, her gaze unyielding.

The sky started darkening as Matt and Emily reached a stone cutout embedded in the massive mountain wall. It was situated hundreds of feet above, overlooking a sprawling valley stretching indefinitely. Ducking through a low portal, they entered what felt like an abandoned lair. The area exuded a mystical, almost eerie aura.

"Must have been tiny Natives who lived here?" Matt mused, his voice bouncing off the stone walls.

"Look!" Emily interjected, her finger pointing towards a cave painting depicting a vast airplane equipped with a radar-like device. A little further away, well beyond human reach, she spotted another painting—a serpent sporting an astronaut's head, painted high on the overhang. "How could the Hopi know about something like this?"

"Bishop probably painted on the side. Lend some false credibility to his insanity," Matt suggested, scrutinizing the peculiar art.

"Come on!" Emily retorted, rolling her eyes at his theory.

"He got up here. He got bored. Ate magic mushrooms. He started making up stories. Then he took up painting," Matt continued, his tone dismissive.

Venturing further into the dwelling, they stepped into what

seemed to be an old medicine man's dwelling. Signs of recent habitation were evident: remnants of a fire, discarded food, and worn-out skins were scattered about. On the back wall, a cave entrance led further into the mountain's depths.

"These hills are honeycombed with secret entrances like this that go deeper down. This could be one of them," Emily hypothesized, peering into the gloom.

"You first," Matt suggested, a hint of trepidation creeping into his voice.

Emily gave him a pointed look before quipping, "Maybe we should knock."

Unfazed, Matt pulled out his gun and proceeded into the shadows.

14

————

The darkness within the cave was near absolute. Emily fumbled in her camera case and pulled out a small penlight. Its feeble glow barely penetrated the inky blackness.

"Professor Bishop, are you home?" Emily called out, her voice bouncing off the walls. Her echo was the only reply they received.

"We read your book. Loved it. We were wondering if we could get your autograph," Matt added, his sarcasm echoing through the cave. There was no reply. They pushed forward.

Suddenly, a torch flared to life, its brightness momentarily blinding them. The man who wielded it, none other than Jason Bishop, lunged at Matt, a warlike grimace on his face. Despite the initial shock, Matt blocked Bishop's attack and responded with one of his own. A quick twist of the arm brought the older man to his knees.

"Why, Professor Bishop, you look nothing like your photograph," Matt remarked, his eyes locked onto the older man's face.

"You never read my book. You're lying," Bishop accused, his voice hoarse.

"And you're not Jason Bishop, are you?" Matt questioned, his tone shifting from surprise to disbelief.

"Depends," was Bishop's enigmatic response.

Matt scoffed, producing a copy of Bishop's book and flashing the cover at him. "Then someone made a big mistake because they put your ugly mug on this cover."

In Warrior Paint, Bishop looked at the image on the cover. It was unmistakably him.

"It's not me. That's not my name," Bishop denied, though his eyes flickered uncertainly.

"Well, what is your real name?" Matt asked, unperturbed by Bishop's denial.

"Nothing," Bishop retorted, his face set into a stern expression.

"An alias. How stupid of me," Matt remarked, turning to Emily, who then spoke.

"Professor Bishop, we're not here to hurt you. My name is Emily Mist. This is Matt Steel. John Lear sent us."

The mention of Lear seemed to startle Bishop. "Lear, he's still alive?"

"If you call baking in a trailer park in 117-degree heat a life," Matt replied, a hint of mockery in his tone.

"Lear said you could tell us about Dulce. The underground base," Emily added, her tone sincere.

"I don't know what you're talking about," Bishop retorted, flustered.

"Then I don't suppose you've ever seen this guy either?" Matt changed the topic abruptly, flashing the police sketch of the alien leader.

Bishop was taken aback, anger flooding his face. "You have no idea what you're dealing with."

"Sure we do. Flying saucers, spacemen, medical experiments. It's old news," Matt replied, unfazed by Bishop's sudden anger.

"They'll kill you," Bishop warned, his voice wavering.

"Just tell us where he is, and I'll kill him first," Matt declared boldly.

Bishop looked taken aback by Matt's statement and sat down to regain his composure. The tunnels around them stretched into the darkness, leading to unknown places. Suddenly, Bishop sprung to his feet and dashed away, disappearing into the cave's depths.

In the fading light of dusk, Bishop sprinted along a ledge of the ancient Indian ruins when he lost his footing and tumbled down. A hush fell over the site as Matt and Emily hurried down the steep stone steps toward their fallen comrade. Matt bent down, pressing his fingers against Bishop's neck. The rhythm of life was absent. The pulse was gone. Flipping the body over, Matt's hand came away smeared in blood. He spotted a bullet lodged in Bishop's back. It was too late.

Suddenly, a bullet sliced through a leaf by Emily's hand. Her eyes, wide with terror, met Matt's. The echo of gunshots filled the air, their echoes reverberating off the ancient stones. Responding to the threat, Matt returned fire and grabbed Emily's hand. Together, they dived for cover, skidding down the rocky incline and into the desert scrub.

Sharp twigs scratched their faces as they made their desperate escape. Then, from overhead, rain began to pour. It was a downpour of rain and bullets, a brutal baptism in the desolate wilderness.

"Rain is supposed to be a gift from the gods," Emily yelled over the storm.

"Some gift!" Matt shot back.

With steady hands, Matt aimed at an MIB agent lurking nearby and fired. Thunder crashed overhead, matching the intensity of the fight. At last, they reached their car, fired up the engine, and accelerated out of there, leaving the bullets to shatter their taillights in their wake. Two black ops agents scrambled into a sedan and launched a pursuit.

Inside their moving car, the rain continued to pelt against the windshield. Tires screeched over steel cattle guards as Matt and Emily navigated the treacherous red dirt road. Suddenly, Emily yelled a warning.

"Matt, look out!"

A deer stood in the middle of the road, frozen like a statue, its eyes wide and reflective in the dim light. Matt slammed on the brakes, the car skidding sideways before coming to a halt mere inches from the creature. The car stalled, and as Matt futilely turned the key, he checked the rearview mirror.

Their pursuers slowed a hundred feet behind them, their headlights flashing ominously. Everything suddenly became exceptionally bright, radiant enough to make it feel like the middle of the day. An enormous owl landed on the hood of their car, causing Emily to scream.

"Holy shit!" Matt exclaimed, catching a glimpse of something massive hovering over their vehicle.

He tried the key again, but the starter only clicked uselessly.

"Emily, the camera. The camera," he urged.

A vast silver disc swooped low overhead, a UFO emitting a blinding white light, its hum a deep, almost imperceptible rumble. Emily brought the Nikon to her eye and started taking pictures.

"What now?" Emily asked, fear creeping into her voice.

"I don't know about you, but I don't believe in 'em," Matt replied.

"It's going to land," Emily murmured.

"Better use the wide-angle lens," Matt suggested.

Without wasting another second, they scrambled out of the car. They sprinted toward a cluster of nearby trees, Matt brandishing his gun.

In the middle of the desert, Matt shielded his face with his hands as the alien craft descended closer. Silently. He fired at it, the bullets having no effect. Emily continued to snap pictures. Suddenly, a high-pitched sound pierced the air, followed by a deafening roar. A beam of light flashed at them, suspending them motionless. They were caught mid-run, floating in a field as though seen in a timeless waltz. Then, everything faded to white.

15

Twenty-four hours passed in an instant. The desert was eerily silent, the previously relentless rain replaced with an oppressive calm. The black Corvette sat in the middle of the field, no more than a hundred yards from where they'd left the road. Unnervingly, no tire tracks marked their path.

Inside the vehicle, dusk was settling in. The driver's door creaked open, and Matt leaned over to wake Emily. Their gazes met – rumpled, scared, disoriented.

"What happened?" Emily murmured, blinking sleep from her eyes.

"I have a pounding headache," Matt admitted, rubbing his temples.

"Something's wrong," Emily said, her voice low and worried.

"We must have hit that bridge," Matt guessed, dismissing her concern. He started the car, and they began to move.

. . .

As day bled into night, they found refuge in a nondescript motel room. Matt flicked on the TV, settling on the Sunday night news while Emily freshened up. They were both high-strung, their skin sunburned.

"Matt?" Emily called out from the bathroom.

"What?" Matt responded, his gaze still on the television.

"Today's Sunday?"

"So?"

"I thought it was Saturday," Emily said, confusion evident in her tone.

"We must have been knocked out after the accident," Matt hypothesized, quickly explaining their lost day.

"We hit a deer," Emily reminded him. She considered this, splashing water on her face before emerging from the bathroom. "No. We didn't hit any deer. We skidded off the road."

"Guess you're right," Matt admitted with a shrug, his attention diverted to looking under the bed. Emily silenced the television, casting the room into an awkward quiet.

"It's happened before," Matt confessed after a moment.

"When? What happened?" Emily asked, her curiosity piqued.

"In college. I was drunk. It was a rainy night."

"They got you, didn't they?" Emily asked, an edge to her voice.

"No one got me. I dropped my keys," Matt retorted, seemingly brushing off the memory.

Emily pulled him out from under the bed, noticing a strange rash spreading across his face and neck. "Take your shirt off," she ordered, her tone business-like.

"Take yours off first," Matt countered, attempting a flirtatious grin.

Ignoring his jest, Emily began unbuttoning his shirt with a determined focus. "What are you doing? I thought we were past this," Matt objected, taken aback.

Ignoring his protests, Emily meticulously examined his face, neck, chest, and back. Spotting a small scoop mark near his spine, she maneuvered him towards a mirror. "Look. What's that, huh? Where did you get that mark?" she demanded.

Twisting his head, Matt saw the tiny red mark too. "It's a birthmark," he dismissed quickly.

"You never had it before, Matt," Emily contradicted him.

"I must have banged into something," Matt said defensively, trying to shake off her concern.

"What did they do, Matt? Who got to you?" Emily pressed, her eyes brimming with worry.

In response, Matt picked up the Dulce Report book that was lying nearby. "No one got to me. Look, all this conspiracy stuff... Think about it. Books, videos, second-hand accounts from unreliable witnesses who couldn't stand up in a court-room. You buy into this crap, and you become paranoid too."

Emily was shocked by his dismissive attitude. "So you don't believe any of this?"

"I believe in the cold, hard facts," Matt retorted.

"Then what are you so afraid of? Why are you so goddamned afraid?" Emily pushed, frustration creeping into her voice.

"I'm not afraid," Matt defended.

"Then what's the problem?"

"There isn't one," Matt said firmly.

"That's what I thought," Emily said, her voice tight with restrained emotions.

"Good."

"Where's the implant?" Emily asked suddenly.

"What implant?" Matt responded, taken aback.

"The implant you had. Amy's implant. The one you had," Emily explained, her tone firm.

"I don't know," Matt responded, his voice hardening.

"Where is it, Matt?" Emily demanded.

"I tell you, I just don't fucking know! Okay?" Matt snapped, flinging a Bible against the wall in frustration. It shattered a mirror in its wake. He began to gag, doubling over and feeling inside his mouth, under his tongue. Slowly, he withdrew the tiny silver implant.

Emily approached him, wrapping her arms around him in a comforting hug. "It's okay. It's okay, Matt. They didn't get it," she whispered, trying to reassure him as best she could.

In the stark motel room, hot water cascaded down Matt's head and neck, steam rising around him as Emily worked to scrub him clean. She was meticulous, rewashing his hair and arm with gentle precision.

Once they were back in the room's central area, Emily moved to close the drapes, creating a sense of seclusion. Matt emerged from the bathroom, a towel slung around his waist. He reclined on the bed as Emily fetched a clear gel for sunburns.

"It's cold," Matt remarked as Emily began to apply the gel to his left hand, lower arm, and a part of his forehead.

"It's meant for sunburn, but it might help," Emily reassured him, her hands moving carefully as she massaged the gel into his skin.

"It could have been worse," she said softly, her eyes meeting his.

"Thank you for being here," Matt murmured, touching her cheek. Emily began to massage his temples, her hands moving gently over his skin. As he leaned toward her, he inhaled the scent of her skin – her neck, her chest.

"We have to take better care of ourselves," Emily commented, her gaze locked with his.

He drew her closer, their lips meeting in a soft kiss that left Emily breathless. Their arms wrapped around each other as their kisses deepened, the two of them sinking slowly into the soft cotton sheets.

The next day, Zeppo was back at his LAPD office, a ringing telephone interrupting his tinkering with the toy helicopter. "Homicide. Zeppo speaking," he said, picking up the receiver.

"It's me," Matt's voice came through.

"Where the hell have you been?" Zeppo demanded.

"Hunting," was Matt's terse reply.

"Great. Listen up. We just booked Josh Logan for murder," Zeppo informed him.

"What? I thought we dropped the case?" Matt said, sounding confused.

"Oh, not on the girl, Matt. It's her old man, the judge," Zeppo clarified.

Matt felt shocked in a phone booth on a Santa Fe boardwalk. "Judge Johnson?" he asked, incredulous.

"Shot through the heart. The prints on the gun matched the kid's. Perfect setup. Oh, and they're looking for you, too," Zeppo informed him.

Around him, tourists moved about, their carefree laughter starkly contrasting with the gravity of the situation. Unbeknownst to Matt, two men in dark suits kept a watchful eye on him from their parked car.

In the heart of Santa Fe, Emily browsed through an assortment of Navaho rugs and linens at a roadside stand. She studied the intricate design on an Indian blanket, oblivious to the two men edging closer. One black ops agent moved towards her while his partner rummaged through their Corvette parked nearby. The sight of the stranger in her car made Emily's eyes narrow.

"Hey! That's my car!" she exclaimed.

The first man quickly grabbed her around the waist in response, restraining her. Spotting the commotion, Matt dropped the phone and rushed toward them.

"Take your hands off the lady," Matt demanded, his voice steely.

"Haven't you had enough fun already?" the agent sneered, glancing towards his companion, who shook his head.

"Can't find what you're looking for? Maybe it doesn't exist," Matt retorted.

"You better come with us. We need to chat," the agent said menacingly.

"My mother taught me never to talk to strangers," Matt replied, not backing down.

"Is that so?" the agent taunted, jamming a gun into Emily's back.

Without warning, Matt sprang into action. He seized the top of a hefty Navaho rug and tipped it over, causing the agent to stumble. His partner rushed forward, only to receive a sharp blow from a tennis racket wielded by Emily. Another carpet fell, and in the confusion, Matt managed to roll the agents up in the rugs. A crowd of tourists quickly gathered, watching the spectacle in awe. The men were trapped inside the carpet, like a rolled Cuban cigar.

"These just don't go with the rest of our decor," Emily explained to a shocked salesperson.

Leaving the scene, Matt strolled over to the agents' sedan, glancing back to see the men struggling to free themselves from their fabric prison. Approaching their car, Matt put bullets into two of its tires, a grim smile on his face.

"Got a couple of flats," he declared.

· · ·

Later that day, the black Corvette pulled into the dusty, one-horse town of Dulce, New Mexico. As dusk fell, they arrived at a ranch with a sign proclaiming 'Vacancy.' Cattle and sheep grazed peacefully in the nearby foothills. Matt sniffed the air appreciatively, the aroma of beef stew wafting through the air.

"I smell beef stew," he commented, a hopeful note in his voice.

16

———————

In a rustic southwest dining room, a friendly cattle rancher in her mid-fifties, known as 'The Mrs.,' ladled generous servings of beef stew onto their plates. Her warm demeanor lit up the room.

"Don't get many travelers this time of year. Too hot for some, too dead for most. But glad you could join us for dinner. Stew okay?" she asked, her voice filled with genuine hospitality.

"Looks great," Matt replied, his mouth watering at the sight of the stew.

"So what brings you to this part of the country? Native artwork, isn't it?" she inquired, trying to guess their motivation for the trip.

"The long weekend," Matt responded, playing along.

"Clear air, too, right?" she suggested with a knowing smile.

"Well, I kind of enjoy the smog. It creates mutants. They add color to the city," Matt said, leaning back in his chair with a half-smile.

The woman opposite him, a character with a sparkling gaze, tilted her head thoughtfully. "Lots of artists in these hills. Folks say they come to buy the art, but you know what I think?"

"What's that?" Matt asked, intrigued.

"I think they come to see those damn flying saucers." Her proclamation caught Matt mid-sip, causing him to almost choke on his drink.

"The flying what?" Matt spluttered out, eyes wide.

"You know what I mean. Up there. Flying around," she said, winking at him conspiratorially. "Place gets so busy sometimes it's like living next to JFK."

Just as she finished speaking, her husband strode into the room. Dressed in ranch attire, General Breakwater grabbed a piece of hot cornbread and shot them a warm grin.

"Missy here telling you her wild stories again?" he asked, chuckling as he bit into the cornbread.

"We only just started," his wife replied with a teasing smile.

"We pay extra to have the military fire off those sparklers. Keeps the tourist trade up, if you know what I mean," the General said, winking at them. He then turned to his wife. "Midge, these folks don't look like the type who believe in that sort of thing, now, do you?"

Matt shook his head in agreement while Emily nodded eagerly. Breakwater's eyes lingered on Matt, scrutinizing him closely. "You know, son, sometimes women have an inner sense about these things that maybe we men don't. You ever think about that?"

"They could be more sensitive?" Matt ventured.

Breakwater laughed heartily. "Ain't that the truth? Things we think about can't be true. Don't mean they ain't. World used to be flat once if you remember that far back. Men would never fly, let alone set foot on the moon. But all that was probably before your time."

Emily, who had been silent, piped up. "Do you ever have any problem with your livestock?"

"Mites, wolves? Things like that," Breakwater answered nonchalantly.

"Anything else?" Emily persisted.

Midge spoke up, "Well, there was that nasty enterotoxemia migrating phlebitis once that practically near removed all the hair off them sheep."

While looking displeased at his wife's bluntness, Breakwater covered it well. "Betcha' there was a lot of disappointed sheepskin car seat lovers in California that year?"

Emily continued, ignoring Matt's discomfort. "What about missing cattle?"

"Em, we're eating beef stew. There's got to be at least one missing cow I know of," Matt interjected, rolling his eyes and losing his appetite.

Emily held her ground. "I'm just inquiring."

"No, the little lady is right. There was one thing. Damn near perplexed the hell out of me till I got to the bottom of it," Breakwater said, pausing for effect.

"What was that?" Matt asked, now genuinely curious.

Breakwater sighed. "It's an ongoing thing. For the life of me, me and the other ranchers couldn't figure it out. So my neighbors say to me, 'General...'"

"He used to be a general. Retired now," Midge interjected helpfully.

"I see," Matt said, nodding appreciatively.

"Anyway, they say, 'General, we got to do something about these cattle razings."

"Cattle raisins?" Matt questioned, clearly confused.

"Mutilations. It was awful," Midge corrected, her face turning grim.

Breakwater continued, "Yeah. So the thing of it is, I looked into it. Thought it was wolves, coyotes, poachers, but you know what, it weren't."

"What was it?" Emily asked, leaning forward in anticipation.

"Don't know. Had the vet examine every which one. No

blood. Nothing. We were stumped for a real long time. Then you know what we found out. It was them damn UFOs," Breakwater concluded, knocking on the wood table for effect and flashing a wide grin. "Don't believe me, do you? Most folk don't. But I could show you if you want to see," Breakwater proposed, his gaze lingering between Matt and Emily.

"Absolutely," Emily responded, already pulling out her Nikon camera.

"It's getting late," Matt protested, his voice uneasy.

"Well, what's it going to be?" Breakwater asked, staring them down with a challenge in his eyes.

Emily readied her camera. A flash of lightning illuminated the room, closely followed by the rumble of thunder.

As the summer storm began to pour outside, thunder and lightning filling the night sky, the trio found themselves inside a large barn. Horses and cattle whinnied and mooed from their stalls, disturbed by the weather. Guided by the glow of a lantern, Breakwater led them to one stall where a vast sheet concealed the dead body of a black Angus.

With an air of gravitas, he partially lifted the sheet for them to see. The sight of the carcass triggered Emily's reflex, her Nikon capturing the macabre scene.

The acrid scent of decay filled the air, causing Matt and Emily to hastily cover their noses with handkerchiefs. General Breakwater, however, appeared calm, his face set in grim determination as he looked down at the carcass.

"Shame what happened. No marks. Nothing," Breakwater muttered, his gaze roaming over the lifeless creature.

"What did she die of?" Emily asked, her eyes watering from the stench.

"Who knows? Vet claims she was drained of blood and lymph tissue just like that. Cut right between the cells," Breakwater explained, his voice carrying a tone of disbelief. "Now, who do you think would be practicing that kind of advanced medicine? Certainly not the New Mexico State Medical facility."

A dry chuckle escaped his lips before he continued, "Yep, word has it you mention the word 'alien' over there, they give you the old ee-lectronic cattle prod. Wouldn't take much of them techniques' fore I stopped talking that crap."

"So, you actually believe in them?" Matt asked, his disbelief evident in his tone.

"Hell, yes, son. I am, after all, a retired four-star U.S. Army general. What have I got to lose now except a few unwanted pounds?" Breakwater responded with a broad grin, the glimmer in his eyes evident even under the fading light.

"I can't tell you how glad we are to meet you. You wouldn't believe what's going on," Emily chimed in, her relief palpable.

Breakwater gave a knowing wink before asking, "Don't tell me. You've seen 'em too?"

"No, not exactly. Have you?" Emily asked, curiosity piquing.

The general cocked his head conspiratorially, a silent confirmation of her question. At this, Matt pulled out his crumpled police photo and held it out to the General.

"What about this one? You recognize him?" Matt asked, watching as Breakwater carefully examined the drawing.

"Oh yes, he's a nasty one. You must be with the police?" Breakwater asked, looking up from the photo.

"LAPD, actually. I'm working on a homicide case. I'd like to ask him a few questions," Matt replied, his tone steady despite the uncanny circumstances.

Breakwater chuckled, "I could show you to him, but I'm afraid you'll have to do all the talking."

The silent exchange between Matt and Emily conveyed agreement - they were in this together, come what may.

.   .   .

Breakwater led them to a barn stall, where he swept away a pile of hay, revealing a steel latch ring. Pulling it up, a trap door was unveiled, leading to a set of wooden steps descending into darkness.

"You first. Down here," Breakwater instructed, his tone leaving no room for argument. Left with no choice, Matt led the way, stepping into the unknown.

17

———

In the heart of the underground foyer, Breakwater approached a stern military guard stationed at a sterile reception desk.

"Give me a couple of them badges, would you, son," he requested casually, receiving the identification tags without hesitation. Turning to Matt and Emily, he handed them the tags with a chuckle, comparing the place to an amusement park - without a pass, one would be promptly ejected. Matt and Emily, taken aback by the surreal experience, obediently clipped on the ID tags.

"How are you able to get in here?" Matt inquired, his voice echoing in the expansive underground space.

"Son, do I look like I just fell off a turnip truck?" Breakwater asked, a slight smirk playing on his lips. "I used to run this place, but one Thanksgiving, I got a hankering for pumpkin pie. So, I told the corps to build me a tunnel direct so I'd be home in time for dinner instead of going through all this rigmarole. You have time for that when you're a boy. But when you're a man, it's just paranoia."

"You come down here often?" Matt queried, his gaze scanning the surprisingly expansive underground lair.

"Why not? These mountains are honeycombed with fantasy lands," Breakwater responded nonchalantly. The general pointed down a long, massive tube-like tunnel, the air within it eerily still. "Down that road, you got your basic missile silos, but since they're dismantling, most of it's declassified now. No big secret. Everyone knows that."

"You said there's an alien down here?" Emily probed, her heart pounding as she mentally prepared herself for the sight that might greet him.

"Hold your britches. That's what I'm going to show you," Breakwater replied, the glint in his eye reflecting his excitement. "Now, a few years back, this stuff woulda' scared the hell out of city folk like you. But now, who cares? Right? We got more serious problems. Like global fucking warming or climate change or whatever you want to call it." His voice trailed off into a chuckle as they ventured further into the labyrinthine tunnel system.

They moved further into the facility, halting in front of a glass inset. Behind the Plexiglas, small gray alien figures lay within cryogenic suspension chambers, eerily preserved like exhibits in a museum. Emily looked at Breakwater. He assented. She took photos, her hands steady despite the chilling spectacle.

"You don't want to go in there. Freeze your knickers off. But there they are. There's your man," Breakwater announced, a note of finality in his voice.

"They're dead," Matt said, his voice hushed as he took in the sight.

"Darn tootin'. More than forty years now. 1947 to be exact," Breakwater confirmed.

"The Roswell incident?" Emily asked, her knowledge of popular conspiracy theories guiding her guess.

"That's the one," Breakwater declared, a hint of remorse in his voice. "We did our best to keep 'em alive, but what did we know about alien medicine? Experts say the atmosphere probably killed them. Hell, I think they caught the Shanghai flu."

"And their spaceship?" Emily continued, her question hanging in the silence of the underground facility.

Several technicians packed up for the night in the dimly lit assembly room, storing away their tools and devices. Matt, Emily, and Breakwater gazed at a mainly constructed metallic disc about forty feet in diameter and eight feet high. Its teardrop shape shimmered with a strange bluish tint.

"We've been trying to duplicate this technology for years. Smooth as silk, lighter than a feather, tougher than steel. Toss a grenade at it, bounces off like a rubber ball," Breakwater said, a hint of awe lacing his words, "Imagine if some third-world dictator got a hold of one of these, we'd be in deep shit."

"Does it fly?" Matt asked, eyes fixed on the alien contraption.

"Why sure it does? Sometimes. Not very well," Breakwater admitted. He pointed out the need for new hydraulics and built-in jet fans, comparing the look of the contraption to the Moller XM-5 VTOL aircraft. Yet, Matt could tell this wasn't the real thing.

"These fans are pretty much silent. But they'll get her up," Breakwater continued, his gaze thoughtful.

"How does it work?" Matt questioned, his gaze fixated on the alien contraption before him.

"Some kind of electromagnetic force field, we think," Breakwater responded, the wrinkles on his face deepening as he squinted at the machine. "Physics is beyond me, but I'm telling you, it's just no damn good yet."

Matt furrowed his brow, his confusion still evident. Emily, however, piped up, "Some people say they have been abducted."

Breakwater shrugged, leaning against the metallic surface of the contraption. "I've heard them stories too. Bunk. You two believe in any kind of ESP sort of thing?"

Matt and Emily shrugged, unwilling to admit to such beliefs just yet.

"Well, the best we can figure out," Breakwater began, his tone indicative of a long-pondered theory, "these aliens, when they were alive, probably had movies a long time before we did. Kind of like a DVD, only with a hologram. You know, full 3-D, surround sound, virtual reality, all that crap. Just like you're there."

As he spoke, Breakwater circled the fake UFO, his fingers lightly brushing over its surface as if trying to unlock its mysteries.

"Well, it seems they used to play these things, and God knows why, but I guess it's just like radio or TV waves. Damn stuff just stays in the air. So folks wake up in the middle of the night, and they're all seeing the same movie over and over again. Ain't that something! And no one knows how to turn the damn thing off," Breakwater chuckled again, seemingly enjoying the absurdity of his explanation.

"And the stories about dead cattle?" Matt asked his tone a mixture of disbelief and curiosity.

"Damn shame," Breakwater sighed, shaking his head. "You give an M16 to a caveman, you think he's going to have problems firing it? Damn right." Breakwater mused, confirming that the aliens, despite their advanced technology, were capable of inflicting harm and death.

"People have disappeared too?" Emily chimed in, her voice barely above a whisper. The echo of her words filled the vast, underground bunker, adding to the eerie atmosphere.

Breakwater shrugged, seemingly unconcerned.

. . .

Moving on, they reached another containment area filled with giant vats of chemicals. Breakwater admitted to their mistakes and the toxic waste its operations created. He gestured to the bubbling vats, warning Matt of the dangers of falling in. With a lighthearted note, he asked, "Who feels like dessert?"

Emerging from the depths of the underground facility into the cavernous barn, the trio brushed the straw and dirt from their clothes. In the gloomy light, Breakwater slid the heavy barn door shut and scattered straw across the entrance, hiding their tracks.

"Kids. You can't be too careful. They like to sneak down there and play," he mumbled.

Outside, the rain still pelted down, though not as furiously as before. As they trudged back towards the house, Emily caught sight of a large shadowy figure. It was a dog, yet its cry sounded eerily like a child's. Its face bore an uncanny resemblance to a little girl. Startled, Emily halted, her eyes wide with shock.

Spotting Emily's discomfort, Breakwater grunted and tossed a stone at the creature. "Go on. Get outa' here! Dog!" He yelled, and the strange creature scampered away with a child-like gait.

In the dusky bedroom, Mrs. Breakwater offered them a tray of warm tea and advised them to take deep breaths of the desert air before retiring for the night. As soon as she left, Emily voiced her concerns to Matt in hushed whispers.

"Matt, I don't know about this place. That dog. I could have sworn it had a girl's face," she said. Matt attempted to brush off her concerns, leaning down to kiss her, but Emily remained perturbed. Her skepticism extended to their surroundings, questioning the lack of other guests in what was supposed to be a country inn. He took a sip of the tea.

As Matt tried to ease Emily's worries, she suddenly knocked the cup of tea from his hand, spilling the hot liquid onto the bed. "Don't!" she exclaimed, "You don't know what's in it?"

Matt was taken aback; he had already taken a sip. But before he could reassure her, the agonized yelping of a Rottweiler pierced the quiet night, ending abruptly with the sound of a gunshot.

He checked his cell phone. There was no signal. Glancing outside the window, Matt spotted a payphone at the end of the dirt lane. Seizing his pistol, he turned to Emily, urgency etched in his features. "Wait here. And keep the door locked," he instructed before hurrying into the night.

18

Matt sprinted toward the phone booth in the pitch-black night, each breath crystallizing in the cool air. He fumbled with the dial, pressing it urgently, but the only response was a disheartening crackle. He jumped as General Breakwater approached, clad in striped pajamas and brandishing a shotgun.

"Who you calling?" Breakwater asked, his voice echoing in the empty night.

"I heard shots," Matt responded, his eyes fixed on the general. Breakwater casually pointed to a fallen telephone pole and a broken line nearby.

Back inside the house, Matt was left alone with an old black rotary phone. His attempts to connect with anyone were futile; the phone rang endlessly into the silence. He was alone. The silence was only broken by his own increasingly rapid breathing.

. . .

Returning to his room proved futile as well. The door was locked from the inside. Despite his persistent knocking and calling for Emily, there was no answer. A cold sense of dread washed over Matt as he barged the door open, only to be met with a room filled with boxes and lamps, dusty and untouched for what seemed like years.

Confused, Matt turned around to find Breakwater at the end of the hall, watching him with an unreadable expression. "Some problem?" the general asked.

"I must have the wrong room," Matt responded weakly, trying to keep his growing anxiety at bay. He continued around the corner.

The hallway was eerily empty and seemed abandoned. The dust-filled air hung heavily around him, and the silence was deafening. He stumbled down the hall, each step stirring up more dust, and the floorboards creaked ominously under his weight. As he hurried down the stairs, they gave way beneath him, and he crashed through, landing in a heap of broken wood and dust.

Emerging from the ruined house, Matt surveyed the dilapidated building. The paint was peeling, shutters were falling off, and the windows were broken. He looked around for his car. It was gone. The silence was broken only by the distant low-frequency Taos Hum amid the chittering of night creatures. The phone booth with the cut wires stood as a grim reminder of his isolation.

A sudden flashback hit him: pulling up to the inviting bed and breakfast house, Emily getting out of the car, the three short gray aliens waving at her, and Emily following them into the barn. He remembered taping and then dropping the implant down inside the car's engine oil dipstick. The memory jolted him back to reality.

"Emily!" Matt yelled, his voice echoing eerily in the night. He raced towards the barn, desperation fueling his steps.

Under the silvery gaze of the moon, Matt tore through the abandoned barn, every breath coming out in ragged pants. Desperate, he shuffled through the straw and hay in search of the trapdoor, but his efforts were futile.

At the far end of the enclosure, a silhouette stood against the ethereal moonlight, arms outstretched. Emily's voice carried over to him, soft and trembling.

"Matt?" the echo of her voice filled the empty barn.

"Emily," he croaked, limping towards the figure. As he neared her, the figure shifted, morphing under the trick of light and shadow. It wasn't Emily but a pitchfork, its prongs raised like outstretched arms. He took a moment, allowing the cold realization to wash over him.

A sound from above in the barn drew his attention. Climbing the wooden wall ladder, he found himself in a loft filled with piled hay bales. His partner Zeppo stood among them, casting a long shadow on the straw-littered floor.

"Zepp, what are you doing here? How did you find me?" Matt asked, disbelief wavering in his voice.

"I tracked you down, Matt. Just like you told me," Zeppo responded, his voice steady.

"Something is going on, Zepp," Matt muttered, his voice barely above a whisper.

"Matt, whatever's going on. It's all up here," Zeppo replied, tapping his head. Matt's eyes fell on a small, glinting object - a woman's engagement ring - adorning Zeppo's little finger.

"Zepp, what are you doing with that ring? That's Amy Johnson's ring. You said she wasn't wearing one," Matt queried, a cold dread seeping into his voice.

"Ahh, never mind about that, Matt. I have friends. They want to meet you," Zeppo deflected, his tone far too casual.

Matt's gaze remained fixated on the ring as he walked

deeper into the barn. Then, out of the shadowy corners, three dark gray aliens emerged, their slim figures starkly contrasting with the hay-filled background. They wore an evil look that sent chills down Matt's spine. He glanced towards Zeppo, only to find the alien leader in his place, wearing Amy's diamond ring and tapping his temple.

Frozen in place, Matt attempted to reach for his gun, but an unfamiliar voice echoed in his head. "You are a good cop. You are safe with us." He fought against the invisible force, his hand reaching toward his weapon.

"Bullshit," he muttered, but his body refused to cooperate.

"Good cops always get their man," the voice continued. The alien leader advanced, its dark, claw-like nail reaching to touch Matt's temple. As the touch connected, Matt's world spiraled into darkness.

19

———

As Matt regained consciousness, his surroundings were shrouded in blurry shadows, and a nauseating stench permeated the air. He wrinkled his nose in disgust, the acrid smell bringing bile to his throat. A disembodied voice, authoritative and distinguished, cut through the thick air.

"Don't worry. It'll wear off," the voice said, its owner emerging from the shadows. The tall man was in his mid-sixties, the head of the newly reconstituted Majestic-12, a clandestine organization supervising alien affairs. He looked every bit the business executive - graying hair, a tanned complexion, exuding an air of power and influence.

"Where's Emily?" Matt questioned, focusing his blurry vision on the figure before him.

"She's quite all right. Decent of you to ask about her, though," the man retorted, a faint hint of amusement in his voice.

"Who the hell are you?" Matt demanded, struggling to keep his tone steady.

"I just happened to be the person who rescued you from

your terrible nightmare. You should be grateful," the man, MJ, answered calmly.

"I'm not," Matt replied with a scowl.

"I'm sure you will be, Detective. And I must commend you on your persistence. I am afraid, however, that you have unfortunately reached the proverbial end of the line," MJ informed him, a subtle undertone of satisfaction in his voice.

"So what's next? We going to play the proverbial 'Name that Tune?'" Matt retorted, trying to mask his rising fear with humor.

"Oh, clever, Detective Steel," MJ said, setting Matt's ID and badge aside.

"Glad we're on a first-name basis."

"You see, we know exactly who you are, Detective. What we don't know is what you've done with our property," MJ continued, his gaze locked onto Matt.

"I sold it to the Chinese," Matt shot back, an empty bravado in his voice.

"I don't think so. During your shoddy and haphazard investigation, you accidentally removed a small silver implant from the victim's body," MJ informed him, his voice remaining impassive.

"Who says it was accidental?" Matt interjected, his mind racing for a way out.

"Indeed, anyway, we don't like to have these items lying about," MJ continued, unfazed by Matt's interruption.

"You looked everywhere for it?" Matt asked, attempting to gain some control over the conversation.

"We left no stone unturned. Now, suppose you tell me where it might be," MJ suggested, his eyes never leaving Matt's.

"Suppose you tell me who you are, and then maybe I'll let you know where it is," Matt retorted, knowing he had little to barter with.

"You haven't much to bargain with, but not that it matters

since you'll never get out of here alive," MJ said, an ominous tone creeping into his voice.

Matt quickly glanced around the room, noting the securely locked doors. "You mean I'll have to spend the next fifty years with you?" he quipped, attempting to hide his rising panic.

"You, Detective, are like one of those old hunting dogs that sniff around just a little bit too much. That curiosity can get you into serious trouble," MJ mused, a cold smile on his lips.

"It's saved my ass a few times," Matt shot back, his resolve hardening.

"I'm sure that has had a global impact. The point is you are in way over your head, and now you are basically dispensable," MJ stated matter-of-factly.

"I thought you wanted the implant," Matt argued, not ready to give up just yet.

"Oh, don't worry, we'll get it," MJ reassured him, his confidence unwavering.

"What if I've already turned it over to the New York Times?" Matt challenged, trying to keep his voice steady.

"We own the New York Times and most of the other unbiased news services you are so accustomed to reading for your version of the so-called truth. CNN, MSNBC, Fox. Without good media relations, how could we have become so powerful?" MJ revealed, a smirk curving his lips.

"Advertising," Matt answered dryly, his comment hanging like a curtain dropping on their ominous exchange.

Matt's eyes widened as the alien commander stepped into the room. This was the first time he'd truly observed one of these gray beings alive, in motion, and under the fluorescent lights in the underground room. The sight was nothing short of sobering.

"I can handle this," said MJ, stepping forward.

"You waste time. Get it," replied the Alien Commander, his voice a guttural rasp.

"Knitting circle begins in five minutes?" Matt attempted a joke, but his nerves wound tight.

"Cute, detective," MJ answered dryly.

"They make a better sweater than your mom, I'll bet?" Matt retorted, attempting to goad MJ.

"You have a way of getting on a man's nerves," MJ snapped back.

"I've been told. So, you guys work together?" Matt inquired, his gaze flicking between MJ and the alien.

"To put it bluntly, we have a relationship. We wash their back. They wash ours," MJ replied tersely.

"That's a lot of bathwater for a secret relationship," Matt noted.

"My dear friend, you don't really think humankind has lived on this planet for thousands of years, and then for some unknown reason, within a span of a few short decades, we've practically reinvented the entire planet in every field from nuclear medicine to space, lasers, quantum physics, nanotechnology to genetics? And we did it all by ourselves?" MJ queried, his gaze fixed on Matt's stunned expression.

Pieces of the puzzle began to click into place in Matt's mind. "So you cheated on the test?" He ventured, his tone accusatory.

"A little scholarly tutoring never hurt," MJ responded, not bothering to deny it.

"What's in it for them? A chance to screw the primitive caveman and his woman? Is that what they get in return?" Matt asked, his voice edgy with revulsion.

"You don't want to know," MJ dismissed him, his tone condescending.

"No, I do. I'm really curious. I've come this far. I want to know," Matt insisted, his determination clear.

"Let me just say we gave them what we give every immigrant who lands on our democratic shores: the Constitution and the Bill of Rights," MJ said cryptically.

In a flash, Matt had MJ pinned against the wall. "You mean government protection?" He asked, his voice laced with anger.

"Naturally," MJ replied calmly, not struggling against Matt's hold.

"And the right to bear arms... very advanced arms?" Matt pressed on, his grip tightening.

"Beyond your wildest imagination," MJ responded a glint of satisfaction in his eyes.

"Freedom of speech, religion, freedom to do whatever the hell they want?" Matt asked, choking him now.

"Don't be a fool. We had no other choice," MJ gasped, his eyes watering from the pressure.

"Why not? Why the hell not?" Matt demanded, his face inches away from MJ.

"Because, Detective, and maybe you can get this through your very primitive thick skull. They are more powerful than us," MJ answered, his gaze resolute.

Matt turned to face the gray alien commander, the reality of the situation slowly sinking in. His world had been upended in the space of a few minutes. The alien leader entered and stepped further into the room, flanked by two escorts. He wore a shiny ring that drew Matt's attention.

"More powerful than Amy Johnson?" Matt asked, his voice barely a whisper.

"I'm afraid so," MJ confirmed, his voice carrying a note of resignation.

"And a federal judge?" Matt inquired, his voice gaining strength.

"He had to be stopped. He was getting close. The boyfriend was convenient," MJ confessed, a hint of regret in his voice.

At this, Matt pulled out his handcuffs and strode toward the alien leader. The alien commander, the top-ranking being on the other side, signaled for his escorts to hold back, allowing Matt to play out his hand.

"I have a job to do," Matt said, the determination back in his voice. Everyone in the room seemed amused. Matt cuffed the alien, who seemed moderately interested in this peculiar human practice.

"You have the right to remain silent. Anything you say can and will be used against you in a court of law. You have the right to an attorney," Matt read the alien its rights, his tone stern.

"Detective, he knows the rest," MJ interjected, his tone dismissive.

"I just want to see him get a fair trial," Matt insisted, beginning to lead the alien away.

"You don't really think you can get away with this, do you?" MJ asked, his expression incredulous.

"I'm a cop. It's my job," Matt responded, holding his head high.

"Well, you're not a very good cop," MJ retorted, a malicious grin on his face.

"At least I'm not a traitor," Matt shot back, his words stinging.

"None of us are," MJ defended, his tone unapologetic.

"Who authorized you to do this?" Matt demanded, stopping in his tracks.

"It comes from the top," MJ replied, his expression serious.

"The President of the United States?" Matt questioned, his mind racing.

"I said the top. It was a decision made a long time ago," MJ clarified, his gaze fixed on Matt's.

"Who?" Matt asked, his voice barely above a whisper.

"Them!" MJ exclaimed, pointing at the aliens.

"And you let them?" Matt asked, his tone incredulous.

"What does it matter to you? They were dying. They needed to reproduce," MJ explained, his tone matter-of-fact.

"You sold us out?" Matt accused, his voice full of betrayal.

"They would have come anyway, with or without our permission," MJ defended, a note of resignation in his voice.

"And in exchange, we get what, advanced weapons systems?" Matt inquired, a hint of cynicism in his tone.

MJ nodded, confirming Matt's worst fears. "Where do you think brilliant ideas come from... outer space?" He asked, a smirk playing on his lips.

"And what happens when the American people find out?" Matt asked, his gaze unwavering.

"They already know through Project Disclosure. Little by little, drip, drip, drip. What could they do about it anyway? Write to their congressman?" MJ chuckled at his joke. "No. I'll tell you. Nothing. Absolutely nothing," he concluded.

"You're wrong about that," Matt retorted, standing tall.

"Detective, people are too busy these days, too erratic, conflicted, disorganized, too fractured, too hungry, too confused, fighting crime, saving trees, bashing the president, pinching pennies, fighting climate change. They don't know who to turn to any longer. Don't you see? They need a savior. In fact, they yearn for one. A new kind of leader," MJ reasoned, his gaze shifting to the alien commander.

"If you're so sure of that, why don't you leave that up to them?" Matt challenged his gaze, meeting MJ's.

MJ laughed out loud at Matt's statement.

"A nation of misguided, self-motivated cynics? What a devastating force to unleash on the universe! Perhaps you forgot something, Detective. We were the ones who got us into this in the first place," he said with a grim smile.

"Your days are numbered," Matt threatened, his tone dark.

"As we all are," MJ agreed, a hint of sadness in his voice.

"The people of this country are a lot more resourceful than you know. The last thing we're going to do is roll over for scum like this," Matt said, shoving the alien.

"I'm afraid, in this case, Detective, that's exactly what we will do. You see, they were here before us. We are the aliens, the interlopers, the invaders," MJ revealed, his voice carrying a note of resignation.

Stunned, Matt studied the aliens. "So, why did they leave?" He asked, his mind reeling.

"Oh, they never left. You see, they... well, how shall I put it? They are us," MJ said cryptically.

"Us?" Matt asked, shocked.

"Yes, detective, let me introduce you to your great, great, great ancestors," MJ said, gesturing to the aliens.

At this, the alien leader rotated his wrists right through the metal of the handcuffs. They snapped open, clattering to the floor. The alien extended his hand for a handshake. Matt stood there, shocked to the core.

20

Suspended upside down, stripped, and screaming, Detective Matt Steel dangled like a piece of meat on a slaughterhouse rack. Aliens prodded him with their cold, shiny devices. The chamber of horrors was a smoke-filled space, a spectacle of porous walls and steam vents.

"Where's Emily? What have you done to her?" Matt demanded, his voice echoing off the concrete walls.

Standing beside the alien leader, MJ watched with a hint of satisfaction as the aliens began wheeling Matt towards an amber vat, its fluid bubbling ominously. "You see, Detective, they really are a very friendly people," he commented dryly, his eyes never leaving Matt.

Matt's response was to shout back, "You son of a bitch!"

As Matt was lowered into the vat, his body began to sizzle. They kept him submerged until his movements ceased and then hoisted him back out. Matt's hair had burned off completely, and his clothes were reduced to scorched, ragged scraps.

The alien leader lowered Matt to his eye level. MJ observed the whole process with a twisted sense of satisfaction. "Just one more missing person. What a pity," he mused, causing the alien leader to emit a sound that could be interpreted as a chuckle.

Just as the leader was about to strike Matt's forehead with a lit glass prod, General Breakwater burst in. "Wait! You got your visitors landing in fifteen minutes," he called out.

MJ's eyes flashed with a predatory grin. "Yes, so why waste such a fine genetic specimen?"

Matt was alone and pinned like an insect in a small, oval-shaped examining room under a harsh, bright light. The remnants of his hair were gone, leaving his head bald and his eyebrows nonexistent.

The door slid open, and a female alien walked in, clad in a glowing white gown and armed with a powerful laser weapon. She was taller and thinner than the others and had the same soulless dark eyes. Yet, her lips seemed to radiate a kind of sensual smile despite their motionlessness.

"Touch my arm," she commanded.

Matt strained against the invisible force holding him down, but it was futile. He was frozen in place.

Despite her chilling appearance, his interrogator began to massage his temples softly. "Where's Emily?" Matt managed to ask, his voice hoarse.

"She is unharmed as long as you cooperate," the alien replied, her voice oddly soothing.

His body aching, Matt could not hide his relief as the alien woman wiped him down with a damp cloth, easing his pain.

"It feels good if you just let go," she encouraged, her voice seemingly emanating from inside his head. It was soft, hypnotic.

"I can't," Matt whispered, his voice shaky.

"This is not your first time," she said. "Long ago. As a boy. Don't you remember? I was with you."

"What are you talking about?" Matt asked, confusion mingling with his fear.

"You tried so hard to forget me," she continued, ignoring his question.

As her hand traveled to his stomach, then slipped under the towel at his waist, Matt tried to contain his fear. "You're not exactly Miss Universe," he snapped, desperate to distract himself from the strange sensation.

"I can be anything you want me to be," she replied, her voice low and seductive.

"How about out of here?" Matt retorted, his tone grim.

"Just close your eyes and dream," she suggested, her fingers tracing an intimate path up his thighs.

"Why are you doing this?" Matt asked fear, frustration, and a hint of excitement bleeding into his words.

"Because I love you," she responded, her voice a whisper in his mind.

As she pressed a button, the table Matt was lying on tilted down, allowing her to climb on top of him. She let her gown fall to the floor, leaving her naked. She began a gentle rocking motion, side to side, back and forth, gradually gaining in intensity.

Her large, inky black eyes bored into Matt's, probing deeper and deeper. She opened her thin mouth, her tongue slithering to touch her dark lips as she moved in for a kiss. Matt revolted, twisted his head to the side, and clenched his teeth.

"My momma told me nice boys never kiss on the first date," he spat out, his voice filled with disgust.

"Your mother was wrong," the female alien responded, her voice chilling. "You are under my control now."

"Fuck you!" Matt countered with venom.

In a swift motion, the alien rose, anger emanating from her. She reached for the light gun. For the first time, Matt saw her for what she truly was: a hideous monster. The spell that had held him was broken. Something deep within him stirred, and he erupted into action.

With a sudden burst of strength, he snatched the light gun from her grasp. He locked his arm around the alien's neck and wrestled her to the floor with the light gun pressed against her throat.

"How can you do this?" the alien cried, disbelief in her voice.

"I faked it," Matt shot back, adrenaline pumping through his veins. He scrambled for his jacket and pants. Keeping the light gun barrel pressed against the alien's skull, he quickly pushed her towards the door.

"Now, let's go tell your little buddies," he said, his voice as hard as steel.

"Tell them what?" the female alien queried, her voice shaky with fear.

"Earth boys don't like being fucked," Matt responded, his voice brimming with a cold, determined fury.

21

———————

The alien female tried to call out, but Matt clamped his hand over her mouth. He could hear her cries in his mind and jammed the gun harder under her chin. "Don't even think about screaming, princess," he warned, his tone threatening. She implored him, her eyes wide with fear.

"Where are we going?" Matt queried, "I'll tell you where we're going. You're going to take me to your leader." Her head lowered, her eyes downcast. "I never said it was funny," he reminded her, his voice filled with a hard edge.

A human military guard spotted them and pulled out his gun. Fire was exchanged, but Matt managed to stun the guard with his powerful light weapon. A second guard appeared, assumed a shooting stance, but held his fire. "I wouldn't if I were you, pal," Matt threatened, "Otherwise, they'll lose their queen bee. Now, just put it down."

The guard obeyed, placing his gun on the floor. Matt closed in on him, relieving him of his magnetic door pass. He opened a tech closet and locked the guard inside, then turned his attention back to the female alien. "Now, suppose you tell me where they are, cutie pie?" Her eyes darted nervously, but her thoughts betrayed her. Matt had the power to read their minds, a unique ability he had just rediscovered. "Oh really? I'll be sure not to look there."

The room they entered was filled with what appeared to be sperm banks, fertility chambers, and jars containing fetuses. Alien doctors, clad in medical garb, stood over a woman on a table, a procedure in progress. One doctor was about to insert a fetal implant into the woman's uterus. The woman on the table was Emily.

Matt burst into the room with the alien female in tow, the light gun pressed to her head. "Operation's over, Doc," he declared, sealing the door behind him. The alien doctor tried to maintain control, "Everything is under control now. Put the gun down."

"Might want to transmit on another frequency, Doc," Matt retorted, "That channel's blocked."

The female alien whispered, trembling, "He will not obey."

"Once a troublemaker," Matt replied with a smirk. He circled the room, making uncertain and threatening moves, surveying everything. He spotted Emily on the table, a fetal implant ready for insertion. "Away from the table, Dr. Kildare," he warned the doctors, "Or your little drones will lose their queen. And I wouldn't want to do anything to wreck your hive."

The alien doctor tried to argue, "The others are coming," he said, panicking.

"Won't they be disappointed?" Matt retorted sarcastically. The alien doctor continued to plea, "Let her go now!" but Matt was unyielding.

"Isn't that amazing?" he quipped, "Even my parents couldn't tell me what to do. You think I'm going to listen to you?"

"You are among friends," the alien doctor attempted to reassure him.

"Really? I'll keep that in mind," Matt said, doubt evident in his voice. He moved to Emily's side and began to unstrap her wrists and ankles. "Time to wrap up your little science project, doc."

Unbeknownst to Matt, the doctor was levitating a hypodermic needle by mind control. It floated off a table just above the floor, then rose behind him, poised to strike. But Matt saw the needle's reflection on a light reflector and spun just in time. The needle plunged into the female alien's neck instead. She fell to the floor as the others stood, stunned.

"Not a lethal dose, I hope?" Matt asked, aiming the gun at them. "We must help her," the alien doctor pleaded.

"As soon as you wake Emily up," Matt demanded. The doctor complied, giving Emily a shot to wake her. Matt trained the light weapon at the doctor's temple. "Don't even think about screwing up."

"You can read my thoughts?" the doctor asked, astonished.

"Oh yeah," Matt confirmed, "and I can huff, and I can puff, and I can blow your fucking house down. So don't fuck up, egghead!"

Matt's message was clear, and the alien doctor got it. He woke Emily up. Groggy at first, she slowly came to. "Matt, where am I?" she asked, her voice shaky.

"It's okay, honey. Everything's okay," Matt reassured her. Emily tried to sit up and look around. She spotted the aliens and then saw Matt. Overwhelmed, she fainted.

The doctor used a metal wand to revive the female alien. Meanwhile, Matt found Emily's camera bag and his Smith & Wesson. It was loaded. "I want to know what happened to the girl," he demanded.

"What girl?" the alien doctor questioned, feigning ignorance.

"Pickle Breath, I'm talking about Amy Johnson, who died in her sleep. I want to know what went wrong?" Matt insisted, his voice rising with anger and determination.

The alien averted his gaze as Matt shoved the barrel of the

semi-automatic against the female alien's throat. "Is she the only one you have?" he demanded, his voice hard as steel. He released the safety and cocked the gun. "You want to see what a primitive weapon will do to her skull?"

The doctor's eyes flickered to a near-empty row of tubes in a frozen, steaming structure. "All right!" he capitulated, fear evident in his voice.

"That's better," Matt responded with a cruel smile.

"It was a mistake. He was careless," the doctor admitted.

"Who?" Matt asked, his eyes narrowing.

"The shock of putting her back," the doctor revealed.

Matt held up the alien drawing. "This guy? This bastard? Was it him who put you up to this?" he asked, his voice trembling with rage.

The doctor froze, unable to respond. Matt broke the silence with a munitions round that shattered glass vials and steaming tubes. "No one put us up to this. We are allowed," the doctor finally managed to say.

Suddenly, the door exploded open. Armed military police charged in, their guns trained on Matt. General Breakwater, a solid figure in uniform, drove through the center like a tank on a battlefield. "Well, son, now you've seen the whole shooting match," he called out, "So, do you want to be a hero, or do you want to be smart?"

"I'd like to do both," Matt retorted, unfazed. With an amused expression, Breakwater surveyed Matt's weapons, the laser light gun and the Smith & Wesson 9 mm. His men only had conventional arms.

"Arrest him, boys," Breakwater ordered. As Matt raised the light gun toward them, they stopped dead in their tracks. "You don't know how to use it," Breakwater challenged.

"Ask your nice boys in the hall," Matt replied, "You see, I'm walking out of here, General. And I'm taking Amy Johnson's killer with me."

"Sure, you are. No problem with that," Breakwater responded, an arrogant smile playing on his lips, "Just who do you think you're messing with, son? A bunch of yahoos from Mars? This ain't no sideshow at the circus. This is the real goddamned thing."

"You turn the guy over, or I'll see you all in hell," Matt warned, his voice deadly calm.

Outside, in the darkness of the night, a UFO touched down on the ranch.

22

———————

Inside the operating room, tension filled the air. Matt held the laser rifle aloft while a private rushed to Breakwater's side. A distant warning alert pierced the quiet night.

"They're here for the pick-up," the private informed Breakwater, his voice shaking slightly.

"What's it going to be, son?" Breakwater challenged, eyeing Matt. The military police cocked their weapons, their fingers itching at the triggers.

Matt stood defiantly in front of the aliens' rare collection of bottled fetuses and other genetic oddities, ready to unleash the power of his weapon.

"No. Stop! It will set us back decades. We are already behind," the alien doctor protested, realizing the potential damage Matt could inflict.

"You'd better get away from there, son," Breakwater advised with a hard edge in his voice, but Matt remained unmoved. Irritated, Breakwater motioned for one of his men to remove Matt.

"I'll shoot," Matt warned, his voice icy. And he did, the shot ringing out and striking the military police officer in the leg.

Just then, MJ returned. "Well, well, lieutenant. Perhaps I

overestimated our visitors' ability to penetrate *your* thoughts?" he said with a dry laugh.

"I have a very thick skull, and I don't like being told what to do or how to think," Matt retorted, his tone equally mocking.

"Evidently," MJ conceded. He turned to Breakwater.

"What do you want me to do with the sonofabitch?" Breakwater asked.

"Give him what he wants, of course," MJ said, earning him a disbelieving stare from Breakwater.

No more alert, slightly amused, Emily took a few photos of the unfolding drama.

"I beg to differ here, sir, but we can't just let him walk out of this place. The least we could do is wipe his memory," Breakwater protested.

MJ merely shook his head. "I think you're forgetting something, General. The detective evidently has an airtight case against his suspect. And, with so much unreturned evidence out there, it could present a small problem."

The alien leader was escorted in, still wearing Amy's ring. Matt bristled with the urge to hit the alien, nearly overwhelming him. But he maintained control, turning to MJ. "I'll show you where the implant is," he said.

"Fine. How primitive. Then, let's get on with it," MJ replied dismissively.

Before they could depart, the chief alien Commander moved closer with two alien escorts. The guards carried laser rifles similar to Matt's weapon. He was clearly outgunned now. The alien Commander scanned the room, his voice filling the space. "What is going on?"

"This is the gentleman who has so carefully hidden your lost probe," MJ explained, gesturing towards Matt.

The alien Commander moved towards Matt, examining him from head to toe before looking deeply into his eyes. He then turned his gaze to Emily. "Erase them," he ordered, his voice dripping with authority.

MJ retorted to the alien Commander's decree, "Commander, I think you're forgetting something. If anybody finds the implant, we could have a lot of explaining to do."

"They will not know what it is," the Commander countered, unfazed.

Matt, seizing the moment, moved to his human counterpart, MJ. Placing a hand on MJ's shoulder, he faced the alien Commander. "Commander, I think this human vomit pit has a very good point," he spat out the words with a defiance that filled the room.

"If I have to face a congressional committee on this issue, the outcome would be ruinous for both of us," MJ said, his voice steady. "We would have red tape up the proverbial yin-yang, and we could no longer guarantee your personal safety and privacy."

After a long pause, the alien Commander sighed. He looked around the room at the assembled military, aliens, and humans. "Inferior life forms. Abort them!" he ordered, prompting his escorts to raise their advanced laser weapons.

Before the human military police could respond, laser blasts flew toward Matt and Emily. In the ensuing chaos, Matt dove behind a bank of fetuses while glass and embryos exploded all around. Firing back, he managed to kill one of the alien escorts, but MJ stepped in to halt the altercation.

Without warning, General Breakwater turned on MJ, shooting him right through the chest, then engaged Matt in a violent struggle. Amid the chaos, the alien doctor pleaded, "Stop. Do not shoot the babies!"

A laser blast cut through the glass, liquid, and tissue vials, striking down the doctor. The room filled with gunfire as Matt, the aliens, and the military police fought it out. Amid the chaos, Emily reached for her camera and continued snapping photos.

Just as Matt reloaded, a military policeman released a smoke grenade and moved in on him. "Just whose side are you on?" Matt challenged, rolling out of the way as a bullet whizzed past him. Emily came to his rescue, sticking a needle into the officer's leg. As the officer's face met an acid vat, Matt grabbed his weapon and joked, "Try the pea soup next time, pal."

He tossed the light gun to Emily and instructed, "Cover me," as he skirted around the room. Taking a bullet, he kept firing until his ammunition ran out. He crawled toward a cabinet to grab a knife. The alien Commander stepped on his hand.

"You cannot get up," the Commander stated, a glimmer of satisfaction in his eyes.

Matt said, "You're right. I can't."

Matt made a quick motion to distract him. The commander's eyes shifted for a half second just enough time for Matt to gain a mental edge and loose himself from the hypnotic hold. The Commander's brief confusion gave Matt enough time to land a punch that sent the alien sprawling.

The ensuing chaos was a whirlwind of gunfire, blood, and destruction. When the smoke finally cleared, bodies of both humans and aliens littered the ground, and the scene was a macabre tableau of violence.

Among the devastation, Matt found Emily shaking, the horror of the night etched on her face. He hugged her tightly and, glancing at her camera, quipped, "How about one for the front page?"

He snapped a picture of the bizarre scene before helping her to her feet. With her body and hair covered in amniotic waste, he tenderly wiped her clean with a paper towel. "Come on, baby. We're going home," he whispered, his voice full of promise.

23

Just as Matt and Emily, drenched in fluids and covered in shards of broken glass, turned a corner in the sterile military corridor, Zeppo appeared. He looked them over, his eyes widening in surprise.

"Holy shit! What happened to you?" he asked, unable to hide his shock.

Matt pulled out his gun in a reflex at the sound of his voice. "Zepp?" he asked, squinting through the dim light.

"Jesus, Matt. You okay?" Zeppo asked, raising his hands in surrender.

"It's really you, Zepp?" Matt asked again, needing to be sure.

"Yeah, who'd you expect, Goldilocks?" Zeppo quipped, a hint of relief in his voice.

As the reality dawned on Matt, he lowered his weapon. But the respite was short-lived. From behind him, the alien leader staggered towards him, a laser rifle primed and ready. Sensing the danger, Matt spun around. His hand rested a half-inch from the 9 mm trigger. It was a standoff, and Matt's voice dripped with hate.

"Go ahead, scumbag. Read my mind!" he taunted.

The alien tried to squeeze the trigger of the laser gun, but it seemed to falter. Matt, with a triumphant smile, focused intently, preventing the shot. But the mental effort took its toll. The alien fired, and a blast of light filled the corridor. At that exact moment, Matt squeezed the trigger of his gun.

A .9 mm hole marred the alien's forehead when the light faded. Matt moved back towards the lifeless alien, removing Amy's engagement ring from its hand. He handed it to Zeppo.

"Case closed. This is Amy's killer," he said.

Zeppo made a face at the smell of the alien. "We bringing him with us, in my car? He stinks," he protested.

"I thought we could fly," Matt suggested, seemingly undisturbed.

"No way. He needs a bath," Zeppo retorted.

While Matt looked at his companions, Emily photographed the dead alien.

"Think anyone would believe us?" he asked.

"Nah," Zeppo replied dismissively.

Back outside, the dawn was breaking over the ranch. Matt, Emily, and Zeppo approached the waiting sheriff's cars. Over the police radios, they could hear reports of UFOs in the sky.

"How did you find us?" Matt asked, still rubbing his bald scalp.

"Easy," Zeppo replied, pointing to several bright objects hovering high above.

Retreating to the Corvette, Matt retrieved the alien implant from under the hood. Zeppo watched Matt slide the oil dipstick out, revealing the taped implant. His bald head shone in the daylight. Back on the ground, Matt opened his palm to reveal the alien implant. "Now, it's time to discover our future," he said with a sense of finality.

"Think you could fall for a guy with no hair?" Zeppo teased Emily.

Emily took Matt's hand, kissed him, and glanced at the sky. "As long as he's not one of them."

As if taking the cue, the unidentified aerial phenomena, UAP, in the sky began to move erratically before shooting up vertically at an incredible speed. Two F-16 Fighting Falcon Air Force jets trailed behind in futile pursuit.

Emily snapped a photo of Matt, the implant, and the dead alien in the background.

Eventually, their story made the cover of a tabloid at the checkout counter of every supermarket in the country. The headline screamed: "COP BATTLES ALIENS AT UNDER-GROUND BASE," a testament to the strange ordeal they had just survived. Their adventure was far from over.

REVIEW

If you liked this book, please fee free to leave an honest review. Thanks so much.

http://www.amazon.com/review/create-review?&asin=B0CB78CBVF

ALSO BY A.C. JETT

- A Warm Winter Chill
- <u>Abduction</u>
- The Albatross
- The Architect
- Bad Brakes
- Calabasas Hills
- Crash Site
- Desperado
- Earthlight
- Fast Track
- <u>Final Appeal</u>
- Gideon's Fault
- Hal, The Spud King
- Healing Time
- Heartstorm
- High School
- Hypocrisy
- Identity
- Nefarious
- One More Time
- Powder Stream
- Red Ink on Steel
- Sense of Duty
- Shadow Run
- Special Feature Live!
- Stage Fright
- Star Children
- Wanderlust
- Warm Body

AWARDS - SCREENPLAY

Abduction (Body Count)

• Award Winner, Los Angeles Cinema Festival of Hollywood, 2020

• Finalist, New York Short Film And Screenplay Competition, 2017

• Semifinalist, 25th Annual Fade In Awards Drama Competition, 2021

• Semifinalist, Fade in Sci-Fi Awards, 2020

• Quarterfinalist, Austin Screenplay Awards, 2020

• Quarterfinalist, 24th Annual Fade In Sci-fi Awards, 2020

• Quarterfinalist, Screen Craft Sci-Fi Screenwriting Competition, 2020

• Quarterfinalist, Los Angeles International Screenplay Awards, 2020

• Official Selection, Pasadena International Film Festival, 2017

SHADOW RUN

"*Any sufficiently advanced technology is indistinguishable from magic.*"
   - Arthur C. Clarke

In a motel room, bathed in the dim glow of a low-wattage bulb, the wind whistled through the torn valance. It brought a dusting of snow that filtered into the room, settling atop a precarious tower of old newspapers. Huddled in bed, Jack Bradford, who had seen better years, wrote with manic energy. He ripped out page after page from his pad, each discarded idea ending up as another crumpled paper ball on the floor around him. An open bottle of Scotch was within arm's reach, but it brought him little comfort. Solitary, with only his thoughts and the words on his pages for company.

A pile of photographs caught his attention, and he began thumbing through them. One, in particular, caught his eye: a black-and-white image of strangers waving at him from inside the hold of an airplane. It was clear from the picture that Jack had once been a man of great charm. Unnoticed, the soft tap-tap-tap of someone typing filled the room.

Suddenly the roar of an airplane's engines filled his ears, and he stood amongst parachutists, wearing nothing but blue striped pajamas. He grinned and waved at the photographer, then, without hesitation, he jumped without a parachute.

Jack woke with a start, the dampness of cold sweat soaking through his pajamas. He reached out instinctively, but the bed beside him was cold and empty. The lingering signs of a woman's presence filled the room: the scent of perfume, jewelry on the nightstand, and delicate lingerie peeping out from an open chest. Even a walk-in closet filled with clothes. The portrait of a stunning woman dominated one wall, her face obscured by shadows. A strip of black velvet was clipped to one corner of the frame.

"Beth?" Jack called out into the quiet night, but only silence replied. "Beth," he repeated, a note of desperation creeping into his voice.

The scene shifted again, revealing a living room, a picture of neglect and decay. Evidence of a solitary existence littered the room: liquor bottles, fast food wrappers, unemptied ashtrays, and wilting plants.

Sinking onto the couch with a hefty pour of Scotch, Jack lit a cigarette. His sheepdog, Athena, leaped onto his chest, her tongue lapping at his face.

"No, Athena. Come on," he protested half-heartedly, but the dog was undeterred. "You want something to eat? Mom doesn't feed you anymore, does she?"

He refilled his glass, which Athena sniffed at curiously. "No, you don't want this, only for daddy, girl. We'll get you something soon. -- Mom's not coming back, you know."

He downed his Scotch in one gulp, his eyes welling up from the smoke. An orange and black mass caught his attention in the corner – a parachutist's jump gear, a memento of a past life, a past self.

A Few Days Earlier

As dawn broke over the airfield, the chill in the air was palpable, the sort of cold that crystallized breath and made your skin tingle. A crew had already assembled; radio personnel from KLOQ, jump staff from Parachutes Inc., and a hodgepodge of eager spectators gathered around a massive butterfly tent.

Without warning, Jack emerged, now clean-shaven and clad in a shiny black and orange jumpsuit. The crowd erupted into cheers as a small band struck up a lively tune. Hands clapped him on the back, offering congratulations and encouragement.

"Here's morning's Number One man, Jack Bradford," an announcer proclaimed over the din.

A professionally dressed woman, Jack's producer, beamed at him. "How was ground school, Bradford?" she inquired.

"Piece of cake," he replied nonchalantly.

He found his hand being vigorously shaken by a frumpy chairwoman. "You don't know how grateful we are for you doing this, Mr. Bradford. On behalf of Children's Hospital, I can't thank you enough."

He offered a gracious smile. "A pleasure to help out."

A female reporter entered the conversation, running her hand along Jack's smooth chin. "Mmm, I'm sure it is. You getting a little nervous, Jackie boy?" she asked teasingly.

Jack extended his arm, holding it steady as a rock. "Never. Nerves of steel."

Yet, his wide-eyed expression told a different story. Undeterred, he continued his journey through the crowd, exchanging handshakes and pleasantries. The reporter turned back to the announcer once he had moved on, a knowing look in her eyes. "He's nervous alright."

"From twelve thousand feet? Who wouldn't be?" the announcer concurred with a chuckle.

As Jack neared the plane, an engineer secured a portable radio transmitter onto his chest. "I've rigged it so the mic will always be on. You just keep talking, and we'll pick you up."

"All the pieces? Promise?" Jack asked, his tone demanding reassurance.

"Yeah, sure," the engineer replied dismissively.

But Jack persisted. "Seriously. How am I supposed to take my call-ins?"

Meanwhile, a jump instructor had started fastening a buckle on Jack's shoulder. "How's that? Tight enough?"

"Make it any tighter my right arm will fall off," Jack quipped.

"Wouldn't want to do that. You got to pull with your right," the instructor advised him.

"What if I'm left-handed?" Jack asked a mischievous glint in his eyes.

Shadow Run